Last Chance

by

Martha O'Sullivan

ISBN: 978-1-7367667-2-9

Last Chance

Cover by Charmaine Ross

Formatting by coversbykaren.com

To my late parents, especially my mother,
for all the gifts.

The Chances Trilogy
By Martha O'Sullivan

Second Chance
Chance Encounter
Last Chance

Christmas in Tahoe (Coming in 2022)

Visit marthaosullivan.com for summaries, excerpts
and more.

CHAPTER ONE

The shade hadn't been in her sixty-four count, sharpener-inclusive box of crayons, but Moira Brody had known it for as long as she could remember. Saturating the cloudless sky, it hung behind the Sierra Nevadas like a boundless blue curtain, encompassing the milky peaks and snow-clad pines before yielding to the preternatural liquid hue that was Lake Tahoe. Moira's boots crunched on the snowpack as she welcomed the blast of crisp air that replaced the arid closeness she'd been breathing for the last hour. Inhaling antidotally, she aimed her gait at the freshly shoveled path. She knocked and opened the door at the same time. "Linds?"

"Up here."

Moira stomped the snow off her boots, then shed them and her coat before following the sound of footfalls upstairs. The smell of fresh wood and lemon beeswax drew her to the bedroom at the end of the hall. There she found Lindsay Rembrandt contemplating three paint swatches taped to the wall.

"What do you think?" Lindsay asked by way of greeting, blonde ponytail swinging like a pendulum at the back of her head. "Muted Mint, Seafoam Spray or Green Tea?"

"You're the interior designer, not me." Moira walked over to the wall in question, drenched in bright winter sunshine. After a moment's consideration she replied, "Muted Mint, not that it matters."

Lindsay immediately straightened her shoulders and knitted her brow. "Why wouldn't it matter?"

"Because," Moira answered, feeling the inner smile spread across her mouth. "When that baby girl is born, you're going to repaint. You should be looking at pink paint strips."

Lindsay's cobalt blue eyes narrowed with intrigue. "What makes you so sure it's a girl anyway?"

"Gut," Moira told her. "And you deserve a girl. You always wanted a sister."

"I thought I had one," Lindsay reminded her gently.

"You know what I mean," Moira returned in kind.

"Brian and I just want a healthy baby," she maintained, but the delight on her face intensified. "Besides, we already have Kelsey."

"Kelsey's nearly out of college. You could be a step-grandmother in a few years."

"Bite your tongue." Lindsay broke their shared gaze and reverted to the task at hand, giving Moira a profile view of her second trimester baby bump. "Good call with the Muted Mint, though. That's what we're painting the nursery at home. It seems silly to have one at each house, but I feel so close to Gram here. I want her to be a part of it."

"She'd be so happy for you, Linds. And so proud."

"I know." She brushed her fingertips under her lower lashes. "Damn hormones. I don't have a thing to cry about."

"Emily was the same way. And the cravings," Moira went on theatrically, waving her hand in the air. "Jack was forever running to Raley's in the middle of the night."

"How are the twins?"

"Great. I'm babysitting them on Friday night. They're starting to—"

"You're babysitting your nephews on Valentine's Day?" Spinning back around, Lindsay cut her off.

"Yeah."

"With Paul?"

"No."

"Why?"

"Because Jack and Emily hardly ever get an evening out, let alone an overnight."

"Why aren't you doing something with Paul on Valentine's Day?" Lindsay's tone was a mixture of disappointment and confusion.

Moira had wondered the same, but kept that to herself. "He hasn't mentioned anything. And you know how hard it is to find a babysitter on Valentine's Day," she hesitated, then added, "I offered."

"You offered?" Lindsay repeated in open-mouthed wonder.

"Yeah, I stayed with the boys last year."

"But everything was different then!"

"It certainly was. They were barely walking. And you weren't married, let alone pregnant."

"I mean with you and Paul and you know it!"

Moira started with a tired breath, "Linds…"

"Did you break up?"

"No. We weren't really all the way together."

"You looked pretty together at my wedding," Lindsay pointed out.

"That was six months ago."

"I knew something was up. You skirted the issue every time I mentioned it. Shame on me for not putting two and two together sooner."

"Yeah, because between remodeling a house, going back to school and having a baby you should have been more on top of my love life. All while living four hours away."

Lindsay ignored Moira's attempt at sarcasm and taking her hands, said in earnest, "I'm sorry, Moirs. I didn't realize it was so…" she searched for the word, "casual between the two of you."

"Me neither." Moira's heart caught up with her mouth and she finished quietly, "It is what it is."

"And what is that exactly?"

"What it's always been. Friendship. Familiarity. History. Maybe that's all it's supposed to be," Moira told her with borrowed conviction.

"Yeah," Lindsay allowed with a skeptical shake of the head. "Maybe."

"Now, show me the pink swatches you picked up."

Lindsay shot her a measured look, but relented, "You know me too well."

"Likewise," Moira replied, also knowing the matter was far from laid to rest.

*****

"It's not like she owes me an explanation or anything," Paul Webster told Jack Brody later that afternoon. "I'm just surprised."

"I was too when she offered," Jack said from across his cluttered desk. "But I've learned not to ask too many questions of the women in my life. Beginning with my sister and ending with my wife."

Suddenly uncomfortable, Paul shifted in his seat and released a jagged breath. He'd gotten into the habit of taking Moira for granted, he supposed. But not to the tugging feeling in the pit of his stomach when he let himself think too much about her. "Where is she anyway?"

"Up at the lake. Lindsay's in town. They're picking out paint or curtains or something," Jack informed him with a dismissive wave.

"Figures."

"So what's the deal with you two anyway?" Jack asked. "Is it an on-again, off-again thing?"

"No." Paul found himself oddly offended. "There is no deal. It's Moira for God's sake. Sometimes it's just a little weird. Almost like dating your sister."

"Actually, it *is* dating my sister." Jack's hazel eyes clouded. "Don't break her heart or anything. Hate to say it, but blood is thicker than water. Even though you literally saved my life in the latter."

Jack ended on a light note, but Paul noted the nuance of his words. "It's not like that. We stumbled into I don't know what, and then right back out again. Hell, I'm in Portland nearly every week now and playing catch-up in the office on the weekends."

Jack silenced his half-assed explanation with a decided hand. "Emily thought I should talk to you before we made any definite Valentine's Day plans. In case you were planning a surprise."

Paul leaned forward in an attempt to settle the restlessness swirling inside him. "What kind of surprise?"

Jack shrugged. "Dinner, flowers, little gifts. All that stuff I used to do before I got married."

Paul had done all that stuff too…for Lindsay, he reminded himself with a mental kick. But everything with Moira was different. Easy, casual, familiar. Wooing her didn't even occur to him. Should it? He sure as hell didn't like the idea of wooing her occurring to someone else.

"So can I tell my hopelessly romantic wife that we have a night to ourselves?" Jack's eyes danced hopefully.

"Only if she finds another babysitter," Paul heard himself say. "Moira has plans."

CHAPTER TWO

"Happy Valentine's Day."

Moira lifted her eyes from the computer monitor in the direction of the familiar voice.

"Happy Valentine's Day to you." She marked her place on the spreadsheet and pushed up from behind her desk. "I didn't expect to see you today."

"I was in the area unexpectedly. Thought I'd drop by my best account."

"Brody and Sons Construction is your best account, huh?" she challenged around a laugh.

"Okay," Jason Parker conceded affably. "My favorite account. I had a meeting down the block." He took in the open-air office asking, "Is Jack around?"

"Jack is never around on paydays or Friday afternoons. Today is both."

Jason's chiseled jaw relaxed, allowing his loose male grin to advertise his movie star white teeth. "That's right. I've heard how your Irish temper comes out when you do the books."

"Small business ownership is a perpetual roller coaster. Business is strong but supply chain remains a challenge. It's a domino effect."

"Same here."

Moira returned the cordial, lingering smile, but intuition told her Jason Parker had more than windows on his mind. And she wasn't sure how she felt about that. After a few silent beats she put in, "I'll tell Jack you stopped by."

Jason didn't respond, only gave her a meditative nod. Then his expression tightened and Moira could almost see his heart begin to race inside his chest. "So, what are you up to tonight? Big Valentine's Day plans?" His blue eyes swept the office, then rested on Moira's desk as if searching for something. Like flowers. Or a chocolate heart. Or anything to denote Valentine's Day.

Moira willed the heat rushing through her body not to settle in her cheeks. She cleared her throat and commended herself for having the inadvertent foresight to keep the reception counter between them. Then she answered in a voice higher than she would have liked, "Me? Oh, no. Someone has to keep the lights on around here, you know," she told him, gesturing to her desk. "And people expect to be paid, Valentine's Day or not."

That seemed to surprise, then please him. The confident countenance returned and rested squarely on the broad shoulders supporting his suit coat. "How about dinner, then? Everything decent is probably booked, but we could go a little later, after the rush," he offered with building enthusiasm. "That would give you time to finish up. Or we could get take-out and eat it here."

Grateful Jason didn't suggest take-out at his place, Moira began a weak internal debate. Her conversation with Paul the day before yesterday had been brief and in response to a butt call on his part. He hadn't said anything about Valentine's Day or the weekend. Emily had come down with the flu, so she and Jack were staying home. And Lindsay had gone back to San Francisco.

"You have to eat, one way or the other," Jason was still talking.

She met his expectant stare head-on. There was no reason not to accept his heartfelt invitation. "Take-out would be great," she decided out loud.

"Then it's a date," he triumphed. "Think about what you'd like to eat. I'll touch base in a few hours."

Moira pushed back the bittersweet twinges nipping at her stomach and managed an oblique smile. "Anything is fine. Surprise me."

*****

Paul mumbled under his breath and patted his pockets. He must have left his phone in the car. He cast his gaze upward, letting the sun's position on the horizon confirm his suspicions that he was running late. The florist closed at six o'clock, Valentine's Day or not, he'd been told when placing his order. The clerk had also remarked that at this late juncture, his only saving grace was that he didn't want roses. And that was not by accident.

He'd given Lindsay and every other woman he'd dated roses, but Moira was more of a hydrangea or a lily than a rose. Not that he'd ever given her flowers before, he self-admonished as that ineffable feeling began engulfing his gut again. He picked up his pace and arrived at the florist in less than five minutes. The dry heat billowed out into the damp winter air the second he opened the shop door, biting at his cheeks. He got in line and began to mentally review his plan. Every restaurant in town was booked solid by the time he'd tried to make a reservation, but Moira was easy to please and take-out would surely due. The tricky part would be tearing her away from work so close to the fifteenth of the month.

He was ruminating on his midweek conversation with Jack for the umpteenth time when he heard an orotund voice behind him point out, "I think it's your turn."

Returning to the present, Paul threw an apology over his shoulder and stepped forward.

"No problem," the man replied. "I'm in no hurry myself, but the guy behind me is sweating bullets. Once you're in, you're in, I told him. Florists want to make money just like the rest of us."

Nodding in agreement, Paul turned his attention to the person addressing him from behind the counter.

"Picking up, sir?"

"Yeah. Webster."

The perky teenager punched at the keyboard and consulted the computer monitor. "One Spring Splash bouquet, substitute roses." She hit a few more keys, then handed Paul a receipt. "They'll bring it right up."

Paul followed her silent direction and stepped aside. The customer behind him advanced and started with a sigh, "I know it's slim pickings, but are there any red roses left?"

"I'm sorry, sir," the girl apologized with the inklings of a smirk. "We're sold out of red roses, but have an array of other flowers. We could arrange something lovely for you."

Undaunted by what should be a less than startling revelation, the man rounded his cheeks conspiratorially. "Surely there must be something in the back? Even some imperfects? This is a first date; someone I've been interested in for some time. I don't want to blow it."

"We don't discount; the owner is very particular," she explained with a more compassionate smile. "But I could double-check the cuttings. You'll have to wait until I fill all these orders, though." She tipped her head at the dozen man deep line. "It might be a few minutes."

"No problem. She's working late anyway." The man joined Paul next to the near-empty glass door cooler. "I guess cuttings are better than nothing," he said around a shrug.

"I'm sure they'll find you something," Paul encouraged, feeling sorry for the complete stranger. "Might not be red roses though."

"I knew that would be a long shot."

"I wish I could have given you mine. I had them switched out."

"You're kidding," he responded with a jolt. "What woman doesn't like roses? Especially on Valentine's Day?"

"It's not that she wouldn't like them. They just don't suit her."

The man laughed without opening his mouth. "For your sake I hope not."

Just then a woman appeared from behind the counter calling, "Mr. Webster?"

"Right here."

Stepping forward, Paul took the cellophane wrapped bouquet from her hands. "Thanks."

"My pleasure."

Turning around, he shot his new acquaintance a tight nod. "Good luck."

"Same to you."

Suddenly dismayed by the thought he would need it, Paul turned on his heel and walked out into the brisk night. It was full dark now and the headlights gleaming off the wet pavement reminded him of his next stop. He wondered if Moira would be as surprised to receive the gift as he'd been to buy it. But he'd felt as compelled to purchase it as he had been to be with her tonight. He'd held up his part of the deal, whatever the deal was. The rest was up to her.

CHAPTER THREE

Moira pushed her bangs out of her eyes and blew out her third calming breath. She'd flown through payroll before running home to change and freshen up. Now she was back at the office with the intention of reconciling the ledgers. Instead, she was contemplating herself in the full-length mirror on the back of the bathroom door for at least the fifth time. She hadn't wanted to wear the distressed jeans and cotton sweater she'd thrown on this morning, but didn't want to try too hard either. A dress was out of the question and presumptuous, not that she had anything appropriate anyway. So she'd chosen the floral blouse she'd bought on her last trip to San Francisco and skinny jeans with a little bling on the back pockets. The outfit had been the easy part; the shoes were the problem. She glanced from one foot to the other, each modeling an option. Boots were casual and sexy. Heels were stylish and sexy. Both sent a message—a sexy one. But Moira wasn't sure sexy was the message she wanted to send.

She hadn't had a date, first or otherwise, in ages. Lindsay's wedding had been as close to a real date as she and Paul had gotten, Moira supposed. Aside from that it was going here and there, seeing a movie, attending an event or a family function.

None of which were ever followed by anything more than a parting good night kiss.

Except for that night.

That kiss, or kisses, she corrected herself, had been the first time there had been more, much more. The first time the pull in her stomach had crept downward and settled between her thighs. The first time the buzzing in her head had spread to every cell in her body and exploded. The first time the steady canter of her heartbeat became a hastening gallop. But not the first time Paul backed off and said good night. That happened every time.

Not that she would have wanted to lose her virginity in such a wine-induced state anyway, she grunted under her breath. And to all people, Paul Webster, her ninth grade lab partner and brother's best friend. Yes she did, she thought, grimacing at her reflection. But of late Paul had been aloof, indifferent, busy. And in Portland half the time.

Jason Parker, however, the ash-blond, spring ski-tanned, five o'clock-shadowed window salesman was in her office every month. And he seemed genuinely excited about spending the evening with her. And not just any evening. Valentine's Day. A Valentine's Day date. Jason had said so himself. Her thoughts were returning to her footwear dilemma when she heard the door chimes ring. "Shit!" she swore under her breath, pushing down the melancholy. She kicked off the chunky heel and tugged on the other pump boot, then indulged herself with another quick glance in the mirror. Scrunching the teeming curls she'd grown up hating, she squared her shoulders and painted on a smile. But when Moira emerged with a cheery greeting on her lips, she found the office just as empty as she had left it. Except for the artfully arranged bouquet of red roses cradled in white carnations sitting on the counter. She discharged a shotgun breath. This was definitely a date. The rosebuds were small and the stems short, peeking out of the hourglass-shaped vase girdled with a red velvet bow. She was leaning down to sniff one when she realized Jason was standing in the doorway watching her. Shuffling back a step, she threw an alarmed hand to her chest. "Oh! I didn't see you there."

He took the two remaining strides to complete his entry and approached her. "Sorry. I didn't mean to startle you. I dropped those off and ran back out to the car for the food." His appreciative gaze took her in from head to toe. "Happy Valentine's Day, Moira. You look incredible."

"Thanks. You too."

He'd traded his dress shirt and tie for a casual button-down and dress pants for slim-fitting jeans. He was standing within a few breaths of her now with a blank look on his face, seeming to debate something. Like kissing her.

Admittedly only partly relieved when he didn't, she shifted her gaze back to the flowers. "The roses are beautiful. Thank you."

"My pleasure. And my second lucky break of the day," he told her. "By the time I got to the florist, they were already sold out. I talked the clerk into selling me the day's cuttings."

How sweet, Moira thought. That sounded like something Paul would do. For Lindsay. She cleared the past from her throat. "I bet they were slammed."

"As advertised. So was Bernini's." He raised his arms to the elbows, displaying two brown shopping bags. "I took the safe route with Italian. Hope that's okay."

"Perfect. I haven't eaten all day. Where do you want to sit?" she asked, gesturing around the room with her hand. "We don't really have an eating area. Just a kitchenette in the back."

He gave the office an appraising once-over, then rested his gaze on the desk in the corner. "Want to pull up another chair over there?"

The desk was in abeyance, but cleared off thanks to Lindsay pretending she was over Brian summer before last. Being Paul's biggest fan, she'd be furious to know it went to such use. Moira snickered to herself. "Sure."

"So, did you get the books done?" Jason asked, setting down the bags and hanging his leather jacket on the back of the desk chair. A woodsy, gingery scent wafted through the air and formed a steady current under Moira's nose.

"Almost," she answered as they opened the foiled-covered containers. "Payroll is sent and that's the most important thing. I can always reconcile over the weekend."

His eyes filled with understanding and she could almost see the wheels turning in his head. "Do you work a lot on the weekends?"

"Lately it seems. First world problems. How about you?"

"Yeah. Paperwork, paperwork. Or should I say paperless work?But either way, I'd rather be skiing or boarding." His voice trailed off and he pulled two wine bottles out of the second bag. "Which do you prefer?"

"Skiing," she told him, relaxing a little. "My eye-hand coordination is better than my sense of balance."

Chuckling, he glanced down. "I'll keep that in mind. But I meant red or white?" He displayed a bottle of each.

Moira felt her cheeks burst into flame. "Oh," she faltered. "Red would be great. Do you need a corkscrew? I think there's one back there."

"No," Jason declined, producing one. "Got that covered. Just some glasses."

"Sure."

Moira started to walk away, but Jason caught her arm and said, "I'm really glad you agreed to have dinner with me, especially tonight. I was almost afraid to ask."

"I'm glad you did," Moira affirmed, hoping she sounded more sincere than she felt inside. He really was a nice guy. She left him with a closemouthed smile and headed for the kitchen. All she could find was plastic cups, but they would have to do. She considered bringing out the candles they kept around for emergencies, but thought better of it. She didn't want to come on too strong and give Jason the wrong impression. And no matter how hard she tried, she couldn't get Paul out of her mind. What was he doing tonight, she wondered?

So when she returned to the front a few minutes later and found him just inside the threshold of the door, she blinked hard a couple of times, thinking her eyes were playing tricks on her. There were a few seconds of shared consternation as she watched him stand there, rooted in pie-eyed wonder, slicing his astonished stare between Jason and her.

It was a good thing Solo cups were all Moira could find, because they immediately fell through her splaying fingers. They struck the tile floor, one clangorous bounce at a time, then rolled away. Frozen in the inertia of disbelief, she could only let them go and bring a shocked hand to her mouth. It took her three reflective beats to process the flowers in Paul's left hand, the bottle of wine in his right. Then her prickling eyes reunited with his caramel-colored ones. His were stormy, full of confusion and awe. And bygone scars. Guilty satisfaction joined the shock and wound into a tight braid of angst in her stomach. Finally, she stammered, "Paul, what are you doing here?"

"I could ask you the same question," he replied derisively.

There was a long, heavy silence during which Moira fought an overwhelming urge to run away. She was still striving for calm when she heard Jason clear his throat uneasily and announce, "I'll just go grab some napkins from the back."

With a grateful nod Moira waited for him leave, then answered Paul loftily, "I'm having dinner."

"I can see that." His voice clipped. "With whom?"

"A friend."

Paul's sable brows furrowed suspiciously. "I don't know him."

"You don't know all my friends," she told him, sniffing the air.

"Obviously."

"Besides, he's a new friend."

"Dinner with a new friend. On Valentine's Day," he disdained. "How quaint."

"I didn't have any other plans, did I?" Her voice suddenly sounded more pitiful than she would have liked.

Paul's posture stiffened and he closed the distance between them with three calculated strides. "What kind of a friend is he?" he demanded as the smell of anise replaced its outdoorsy predecessor.

"Just a friend," she told him with an assumptive shrug, noticing for the first time that he was dressed up.

"Then what am I?"

There was a moment so quiet Moira could hear static crackling in the air. Finally she broke it. "I don't know. A friend I've hardly seen or spoken to much lately."

Paul's expression softened a little, like he already knew that. And it bothered him.

"I see. So how long have you and..."

"Jason," Moira finished for him, trying to ignore the familiar, intoxicating scent filling the small space between them.

"Jason," he began again, "been friends?"

"He's called on us for the last year or two."

"Oh, so he's a work friend? No wonder," Paul disparaged. "He wouldn't know that you don't like the sauce at Bernini's. It's too sweet." He shifted his gaze to the salad Jason had split between their plates. "And that you don't care for black olives."

Moira raised her chin a notch. "I can pick them off. And no, he wouldn't know that. It's our first date," she countered sharply.

"So it *is* a date?" Paul returned to her with flinty eyes and a corded neck. "A first date on Valentine's Day. How sweet," he sneered. "And to think I was worried about tearing you away from your spreadsheets in the middle of the month."

"Tear me away for what?" she couldn't help but ask.

"Dinner, for starters." Flippant now, he noted the clock on the wall. "It should be here anytime."

Then his regard settled on the bouquet in his hand, as if just remembering he was holding it. He deliberated for a few seconds before setting it on her desk with a resounding thud. "I'll leave these here, seeing how the front counter is crowded."

"Paul—"

"I'll hang on to the Cakebread, though," he plowed over her. "It's too good of a year to waste."

He started for the door, but turned on his heel mid-stride to face her again. "Funny. I never pegged you for roses. Too ostentatious. But I guess I was wrong about that too. Happy Valentine's Day, Moira."

The braid in her stomach unwound into strands of dread as she watched him swing the door open and storm out into the night. Beside herself, she could only stand there in stunned silence, hand on her breastbone and tears stinging her eyes.

"Is it safe to come out now?" came a tentative voice from somewhere in the back.

Suddenly remembering Jason was still there, she spun around in complete mortification. "Yes, of course. I'm so sorry. We just had a little... miscommunication."

"Looks like more than that to me," Jason contended mildly. "Maybe I should go."

"No!" she exclaimed in short order. "Please don't. This is all so lovely. I'd really like you to stay.I mean..." She wrung her hands. "If you still want to. But I understand if you don't."

"I do," he told her quietly, then approached her with eyes full of trepidation. "I just don't want to get in the way."

"You couldn't." Moira noted the weight of his words and shaking her head slowly from side to side, matched it. "Because there isn't anything to get in the way of."

CHAPTER FOUR

The black ice cast an eerie sheen on the road ahead and the glare from the oncoming high beams had Paul squinting as if at the summer sun. The weather was coming in fast and he wondered if Moira had gotten home safely.

Or alone.

Or at all.

He should have gotten her roses. But he didn't. Because she's Moira. Effortlessly beautiful, remarkably grounded, perpetually good-natured Moira. And tonight she was something else. Incredibly sexy. In tight-fitting jeans and a silky top he'd never seen before. With her dark, thick, begging to be touched curls skimming her shoulders. And eye makeup and red lipstick. She smelled pretty good too. Like spring rain and lilacs. All for the guy begging for roses at the flower shop. For someone he'd been "interested in for some time." For whom he had a last minute arrangement thrown together. From *his* cuttings. For *his* girl. Paul huffed out a harried breath. Is that what she was? Apparently not. But he sure as hell wanted her to be. He slammed on the brakes and the SUV swerved, then leveled, sliding into the precarious U-turn.

It took Paul twice as long as usual to get back to Reno with the slick roads. And by then the temperature had dropped enough to turn the spitting rain into steely pellets. A frigid, damp sleet akin to the block of ice that had staked a claim in the pit of his stomach. Turning the corner onto Moira's street, he heaved a half-hearted sigh of relief when he saw no car in the driveway and a hodgepodge of lights burning inside. She was home. Alone it would seem.

Unless they came in one car, he prepared himself through gritted teeth.

Paul knew the garage code, but didn't want to scare her, so he opted for the conventional route. He could see her profile through the slats of the plantation shutters as he made his way up the path to the front door. She was in the kitchen fussing with something, still dressed up like she hadn't been home long. His throat muscles contracted as his mind began to race. Had her date seen her home or had they parted ways at the office? Gone somewhere for a drink after dinner? Made another date? He looked on as Moira stepped back from the kitchen island, arms drawn across her chest, and appraised her work. The fancy jeans sat just below her hips, hugging every one of her curves from hip to ankle and Paul found himself disturbingly envious. The sheer shirt rested on her slim waist and reminded him of holding her in his arms when they danced at Lindsay's wedding. And her breasts looked bigger somehow, like they'd grown overnight. The mere thought of touching them made his heart skip a beat and his cock begin to swell.

Seemingly pleased with her work, she reached for the dish towel flung over her shoulder and dried her hands, inadvertently catching a glimpse of him out of the corner of her eye. She did a double take, then held his gaze momentarily. He thought the corners of her mouth curved slightly upward, but the distance between them was too great to be sure. She shook off whatever she was thinking and walked toward the door. He visualized her on the other side, squeezing her eyes shut and taking a few deep breaths before opening it. She greeted him in a wobbly voice, "Hey."

She looked mesmerizing in the amber light. Her emerald green eyes were soulful and clung to his as if unwittingly attached. Her full lips were naked now and Paul told himself it was from eating. The coal-black tendrils had doubled, the errant strands falling in sexy waves around her fair face. Also from natural causes, he told himself. "Hey. Can I come in?"

"Of course," she invited, ushering him in.

Stepping inside, Paul rapid-fired, "I'm glad you're home. I wanted to—"

"Where else would I be at eleven o'clock at night?" she cut him off.

"I don't know." His mind was suddenly a mare's nest and his palms were beginning to sweat.

"I wasn't sure what your plans were for the rest of the evening."

"I've been home for almost an hour," she informed him evenly.

"Alone?" His eyes scanned the living room.

"It was just dinner, Paul," Moira patronized.

On Valentine's Day, he silently added. "About that, I came by to apologize." He wondered if she sensed the audible relief in his voice. "I shouldn't have assumed we'd see each other tonight. And I certainly shouldn't have assumed you'd be," he bit off the word, "available." He looked away then, into the kitchen, and saw what she'd been doing. Arranging flowers.

His flowers.

She must have acquired clairvoyant powers in those few seconds, because her tone softened and she said, "I had to bring them home. They're too beautiful to waste."

With four long strides he advanced into the kitchen and glanced around. "Where are the roses?"

She followed him. "At the office."

"They're not too beautiful to waste?" he asked in a thick voice, turning to face her.

"No, they are." Her breath hitched. "They're just not from you."

Her eyes were filling behind their dark lashes and she was biting her bottom lip, trying to hold back the tears. Paul couldn't have stopped himself from going to her if he'd wanted to. "Moira, what are we doing?" he implored, gripping her forearms. "What have I done? Have I lost you?"

She shook her head from side to side and the tears began to fall, leaving sooty tracks on her cheeks. Tipping his head back in silent gratitude, Paul gathered her in his arms. She instantly moved into his body, sniffling through sawed-off breaths.

"Tell me nothing happened. Tell me there's nothing between you and him," he prayed out loud after a long moment.

She answered by burrowing her head into his shoulder and wreathing his middle. He felt her breathing level and he kissed the top of her head. She smelled like a subtle version of earlier, infused with wine and garlic. Hope replaced the trepidation in his stomach and he heard himself say, "I had to force myself not to go back there. I've been driving around for hours, going crazy."

She angled out of his grasp just enough to make eye contact. Suddenly she was the girl he used to know again, not the woman tying his insides into knots. Or maybe the perfect combination of both. Her eyes began to shine and a satisfied smile curved her lips. "You have?"

"Yeah. Like outside my mind crazy." He laid his lips on hers and tasted the salt from her tears. She melted into the kiss, then the next. He wondered if she could sense him growing behind the zipper. Or the spool of want unwinding into a thousand frazzled threads in his gut. Gasping for air, he released her mouth and cupped her face in his hands. "You make me crazy, Moira Brody. Absolutely crazy."

Her breath caught in her throat and she swallowed hard. "Then I like you crazy."

Resting his forehead on hers, he let the night roll off his back like sweat. Then he closed his eyes and asked, "Do I need to fight for you, Moira?"

She laughed a little. "Well, Jason did bring flowers, dinner, wine."

"I brought flowers, dinner, wine," Paul defended high-mindedly, straightening. "Did you ever get the Chinese food?"

"Yeah, it's in there." She nodded over his shoulder at the sub-zero refrigerator they'd picked out together.

"It's your favorite. Cashew chicken."

"Thank God," she said lightly, dabbing the outer corners of her eyes. "I'm starving."

Paul sent her a confused look. "Did Bernini's have a bad night?"

"Not from what I picked at."

"Poor guy," he gloated through a chuckle. "Went to all that trouble for nothing."

"I wouldn't say for nothing," Moira demurred, her eyes dancing with innuendo. "He seemed to enjoy the evening."

"Oh?" Paul inquired, stepping out of her embrace.

Beaming now, she raised her eyebrows mischievously. "Yeah."

He felt his expression fall. "Did he kiss you good night?"

"He did," Moira preened.

Paul couldn't believe how much that bothered him. "Did you want him to?"

Her face instantly sobered. "No," she paused, then finished with hushed care, "I wanted you to come back."

"I did." As if he'd had any choice in the matter. Paul drew her to him again and ran his hands up and down her back. "I had to."

"That was all I could think about during dinner," she admitted into the crook of his shoulder. "That I could have spent Valentine's Day with you."

"It's not over quite yet." He leaned back and dried her tearstained cheeks with his thumbs. "Think he'll call you?"

She shrugged matter-of-factly. "Yeah."

"What will you say?"

"What should I say?"

"Thanks, but no thanks." He reached into his jacket pocket.

Her eyes narrowed in confusion as she took the small box from his open hands. "Paul, what is this?"

He gestured toward the bow-topped lid with a tip of the head. "Open it and find out."

Moira obliged as Paul looked on eagerly. A tiny gasp escaped her throat when she saw the diamond studs inside.

"I know they're on the small side, but you aren't one for flash."

She glided her fingertips over each diamond. "They're beautiful."

"Emily thought they were perfect." Just like you, he almost said.

Her astonished gaze shifted upward. "Emily?"

"She's not sick. She found another sitter for tonight." He paused to let the benevolent betrayal sink in. "So we could spend Valentine's Day together."

"Oh, Paul! I'm so sorry!" Moira exclaimed. "I had no idea."

Neither did he. Until just now. And the realization hit him like a ton of bricks. "You can make it up to me tomorrow night," he told her on the fly. "We're going on a date. It'll be our first one."

CHAPTER FIVE

"Mmm. Smells great in here." Brian Rembrandt greeted his wife with a kiss. "Sorry I'm late."

"No problem," Lindsay said, returning to the kitchen island where she'd been putting together a salad. "That's why we kept your apartment, for nights like this."

Brian slipped his arms around her from behind and rested his chin on her shoulder. His grip pushed her thickening middle upward, forming a makeshift shelf under her breasts. "But it's Valentine's Day. Our first one. Officially anyway."

She looked up at him with a weightless heart. Every day felt like Valentine's Day to her. "It's still Valentine's Day. We'll have an impromptu dinner with Mike and Laney. She's officially a San Franciscan now."

Brian released her with a kiss on the cheek, then began opening the bottle of wine on the counter. "That was fast."

"She got out of her lease. And a job opened up in the San Francisco office," Lindsay went on excitedly. "It's a bit of a demotion, but she won't have as much stress and travel."

"Great."

Lindsay was still reveling in having her college roommate next door instead of halfway across the country when a knock sounded at the door.

Brian answered it and a few seconds later Mike Savoy and Delaney Richards appeared. Mike toted a six-pack of Brian's favorite beer and Delaney was holding a platter piled high with shrimp. She deposited the plate on the counter, then took Lindsay into a warm embrace.

"Look at you!" Delaney exclaimed. "You've doubled in size in the last two weeks!"

"I told you," Mike chimed in. "She's gotten even bigger since I saw her last."

Lindsay returned their heartfelt smiles. They made such a striking couple, with their rich brown hair and dark eyes. Filled with true love now, for the first time in their lives. "I'll take that as a compliment. That's apparently how the second trimester goes." She aimed her ensuing words at Delaney. "Just so you know."

Delaney gave Lindsay a furtive look, as if the same thought had occurred to her. Then she winked conspiratorially saying, "Thanks for the tip."

Brian served the drinks while Lindsay unwrapped the shrimp. "Did everything go smoothly with the move?"

"Like clockwork," Delaney answered her, sliding onto one of the bar stools lining the kitchen island.

"I'm just glad she didn't change her mind at the last minute," Mike joked, rubbing her shoulders from behind.

"Oh, stop," Delaney contended. "I couldn't wait to get back out here and you know it."

"I know." Mike brushed her lips with his, then followed Brian into the living room.

Delaney lovingly contemplated his retreating back, then turned her attention back to Lindsay. "What brings you guys into the city this weekend?"

"Brian was working in Sacramento this week and had to go into the office today," Lindsay told her. "I tagged along and spent a day in Tahoe working on the nursery. Moira came up."

"What's going on with Moira? I texted her the other day to tell her we'd set a date, but never heard back."

"Being busy at work would be her excuse for not texting you back," Lindsay said.

"I hear a but," Delaney prompted around a sip of wine.

"But," Lindsay dragged out the word, "I think she's preoccupied."

"With?"

"Paul."

"That's a good thing, right?"

"No. Apparently they've grown apart."

"How so?"

"I'm not sure." Lindsay gazed out the window as if the Bay Bridge held the answer. "Moira acted like it didn't bother her, but I could tell it did," she fretted, focusing on Delaney again. "I have half a mind to call Paul and find out what's really going on. I hope it's not my fault."

Delaney gave her a puzzled look and dipped a shrimp in cocktail sauce. "Why would it be your fault?"

"Because of the way I handled everything with Brian." Lindsay began wringing her hands. "Maybe I ruined him."

"They seemed fine at the wedding."

"That was six months ago," Lindsay echoed Moira's words. "And they weren't even spending Valentine's Day together. Hadn't spoken in days when I saw her."

"Is there someone else?"

"I asked Moira that. She said no." Lindsay turned and stirred the jambalaya simmering on the stove. "Paul isn't like that anyway."

"What could it be then?"

"I don't know. But the past can be a killer."

Delaney grunted. "Tell me about it."

Lindsay spun back around as her brain caught up with her mouth. "Oh, Laney! I'm sorry. I didn't even think."

"Don't be." Delaney waved the apology away. "All of that led me to Mike." Her eyes began to dance as a sure smile crossed her lips. "It was worth it. Exponentially so."

The two women shared a wistful moment, then Lindsay began again, "Enough about me. Tell me about the wedding. Is everybody getting along?"

"Oh, yeah," Delaney replied nonchalantly. "My mom is so laid-back and Tricia has married off four daughters. She's gotten her fix."

"It'll be easier now that you're out here. Let me know what I can do."

"You're already doing the most important thing by standing up for me."

"My pleasure," Lindsay replied from the heart. "My first stint as matron of honor." And hopefully not my last, she prayed under her breath.

CHAPTER SIX

If deciding what to wear last night had been hard, figuring out what to wear tonight was going to be impossible. One thing Moira knew was that she had to go to the mall. She'd slept fitfully if at all and had woken up at first light. Finally giving up on getting any meaningful sleep, she stumbled into the kitchen in her warmest robe and thickest socks and made coffee. As it brewed, she transferred the dishes from last night's late dinner from the sink to the dishwasher. Finding Paul at her door had been one thing; the diamond earrings another. But the most shocking thing about the evening had been his instance that they go on a real date tonight.

She couldn't speak to makeup sex, but if there was a chaste version of it, they'd had it. She'd heated up the Chinese food while Paul opened the bottle of Cabernet that had been rolling around on his passenger seat all evening. He'd made a fire in the living room and they'd fallen asleep in front of the TV for a bit. Moira had woken first and after her eyes adjusted to the light, had to pinch herself. She had, for what was left of it, spent Valentine's Day with Paul after all. He'd left around two a.m. with sleepy kisses at the door. Kisses that held something different. A newfound urgency, an honesty that hadn't been there before, and most of all a promise of something more. Something deeper, closer, more profound.

As the earthy aroma filled the air, she put the kitchen to rights. Wiping down the peninsula island, her eyes rested on Paul's flowers and she let herself indulge in them for a few seconds. Bringing them home had been a split-second decision and had proven more fortuitous than she could have ever imagined. It had spawned a turning point, a moment of truth between them. Leaning down, she inhaled deeply. The sweet, heady scent reminded her of Lindsay's wedding. Of dancing with Paul on the terrace as the waves crashed against the shore and the lake settled in for the night. Of how he'd gathered her close, held her hand, hardly left her side all night. Of their walk on the beach the night of the rehearsal dinner and how he'd kissed her good night so thoroughly before retreating to his room down the hall.

Yet in the six months since, she'd probably spent less time with him than she had in the last two years. She'd been busy, admittedly. Business was booming, her father was spending less and less time in the office, giving her more responsibility and autonomy when it came to making decisions. She'd spent a few weekends in San Francisco with Lindsay and even one girls' weekend in Napa with she and Delaney when both Brian and Mike had been out of town. And of course, she helped Emily and Jack ride herd on her nephews whenever she could. If she really let herself think about it, she'd been more nonplussed by Paul's inattention than upset by it.

Until her conversation with Lindsay a few days ago.

Something had shifted in her then, like it had when she finally admitted to herself that she had feelings for Paul beyond friendship. It had been a slow and unbidden epiphany, not to mention a terrifying one since he and Lindsay were practically engaged at the time. She had shared this realization with no one, as the two people with whom she would usually discuss such matters were obviously unapt.

Once again, Paul was all she could think about and she couldn't blame it all on the Valentine's Day hype. But perhaps the bigger shift had been in him. Last night he'd been forthcoming, vulnerable, honest. And something else—determined, confident, unrelenting in his pursuit of her. Not just that he wasn't giving up, but that he'd realized he couldn't. And that gave Moira an unfamiliar feeling of apprehension and excitement tinged with need. She was not only in love with Paul, she was in lust with him. And she liked it.

Coffee poured, she sat at the island and turned her attention to her phone. If she checked her email now, it would suck her in for hours, so went to her texts. She owed Delaney a congratulatory text, she reminded herself with an inner smile. Mike and

Delaney were as perfect a couple as Lindsay and Brian. And just as deservedly so. They also had to discuss Lindsay's baby shower. Moira would have to involve her mother and Emily in that as well. And of course Kelsey. Maybe make a weekend of it in San Francisco. She answered Delaney accordingly and made a mental note to talk her mother and Emily about it later.

Returning to her home screen, Moira tapped the Facebook icon. *Jason Parker sent you a friend request* topped her notifications, taking her off guard. They hadn't exchanged cell numbers and with it being Saturday, he had no other way to reach her, she supposed. She let out a long breath. How ironic to go from no men in her life to two practically overnight. Now what? Should she ignore the friend request? Delete it? And if he were to ask her about it or resend it, play dumb? There was really no harm in accepting it, was there? Or would that be leading him on? She wondered if you had to be friends with someone on Facebook to message them directly there. She had a feeling that was the end goal here; a follow-up of sorts to last night. They'd had a nice dinner and had ended the evening on a high note, despite it starting off as a borderline disaster. Or maybe she was reading too much into this. It was just a friend request, for God's sake. After all, they had many mutual professional acquaintances. But if Jason's goal was keeping in touch on a personal level and hers was exploring a relationship with

Paul, why would she, intentionally or not, lead him on? That had never been her way and she wasn't about to start now at almost thirty years old. She ran a troubled hand through her hair. Would things be awkward between them now? This is why people shouldn't date people they work with. She hadn't thought that one through.

She decided to shelve that issue for now and move on to tonight. She had no idea where they were going or what they were doing, but instinct told her whatever it was, it called for a dress. Maybe a sweater dress, she thought, looking out the window at the denuded trees and opaque sky. A clingy one. And tall dress boots. Because unlike last night, sexy was definitely the message she wanted to send.

CHAPTER SEVEN

"I'm almost ready. Come in for a sec," Moira told Paul twelve hours later.

"Is that any way to greet a date?" He reached across the threshold of the door and grabbed the handle. "Let's try again."

"Paul, this is ridiculous!" Moira exclaimed, internally amused.

"No, it's a first date. Pretend we met on eHarmony or something." Raising his eyebrows gamely, he shut the door.

After a few seconds of silence, no doubt for her benefit, the doorbell rang again. She opened it, mocking naivety. "Hi."

"Good evening. I'm Paul Webster. You must be Moira."

"Paul, honestly."

"I'm really looking forward to tonight," he barreled over her. "May I come in?"

He looked brutally handsome, standing there in a lavender dress shirt with black pants and a charcoal blazer. Moira's heart skipped a beat, then swelled in her chest as she stepped aside. "Please."

"Hi." Hooking her waist, he pinned his mouth to hers.

Her body began to tingle, the way it had last night when he kissed her good night. But this kiss held something more. It too was full of promise and honesty, but held more relief than urgency. She wondered if he felt it too. She wondered if he felt any of it. "Wow," she breathed. "Do you always introduce yourself like that?"

He clutched her firmly against him. "No, more like this." His mouth captured hers, far from gently this time, and began to feed. Leaving her breathless, he worked his tongue down her throat to the hollow notch above her collarbone. He seemed to debate going farther but instead, inch by leisurely inch, retraced his steps back to her mouth. And when his hands rested on her buttocks, pressing her to him, she felt his desire grow against her, rivaling her own.

And he was barely in the door.

Their lips parted and only short gasps filled the air for a few measured clicks. She watched his eyes fall to the valley between her breasts and linger. Then he returned to her gaze saying, "You look stunning, Moira."

"Thank you," she managed. She'd settled on a dark gray sweater dress, long-sleeved, with a deep v-neck, formfitting but not too tight. Lindsay was always telling her to show off her slender frame and small waist. There was no better time to start listening, Moira had decided that afternoon in the fitting room at Nordstrom. And of course her black leather boots, which she had only worn once or twice before. She'd worn more casual boots last night, not that Paul would have noticed.

"Do you have a coat or something?" Paul was rubbing his hands up and down her arms. "It's cold already."

Her steaming insides altogether disputed that. Her winter coat would take way from the dress so she waved the suggestion away. "I'll be fine."

He considered that briefly, then said, "We'd better head out then. I made a reservation for seven up at Diamond Peak."

"All right," she replied, breaking away. "Let me get my purse."

She felt his appraising stare as she walked across the living room and into the kitchen to grab her bag. Using her phone camera as a mirror, she replaced the gloss he'd stripped from her lips, then momentarily relished in the diamond studs on her ears. She turned off the kitchen lights and switched on the under cabinet dimmers. When she returned to the living room she found Paul looking at the framed photos on the table by the door. "Ready."

He hurriedly replaced the picture of Lindsay and her from the fifth grade and turned around. "Great." He extended his arm out in front of him in invitation, then guided her outside by the small of her back. The sun was setting, cloaking the mountains in pillows of pink as the lights of the valley sparkled around them.

"It never gets old, does it?" Paul remarked, reading her mind.

"No," Moira concurred. "And it seems the older I get, the more I appreciate it."

"Or maybe we really haven't been seeing it until now." His eyes filled with the weight of his words as he held the car door open for her.

"Yeah," she replied around the lump growing in her throat. "Maybe."

They rode in companionable silence for a few minutes. As they began their ascent up Mount Rose Paul said, "Perfect scenario tonight; snow on the hills but not on the roads. At least not yet."

Moira laughed without opening her mouth. "Yeah."

He glanced over at her. "What?"

She turned to face him. "Nothing. It's just ironic that we're going up to Incline. I would never go up the mountain on a first date. Especially with someone I met online."

Paul was quick with a grin. "I guess this first date thing might be harder than I thought, huh?"

"Nothing is hard with you," Moira thought out loud. "I mean," she backpedaled, "it's..."

"Familiar," Paul finished for her. "Comfortable. I know."

They wound through the Washoe Valley and up into the Sierras. Turn by turn, the powdered sugar sprinkled White Firs became massive Jeffrey Pines shrouded in blankets of fresh snow, illuminated by the full moon reflecting off the silvery meadows.

"So," Paul began again, "tell me a little bit about yourself."

"Seriously?"

"Isn't that what you do on a first date? Get to know each other?"

"Yeah, I guess."

"What did you and…"

"Jason," she supplied.

"Jason." He took the next curve a little too fast. "Talk about."

"Our families. The industry. The economy."

"Okay, then. Tell me about your family. Do you have siblings?"

"Paul—"

He held up an index finger. "Ah, ah, ah. First date, remember?"

It would be kind of fun to play along, she supposed. "I'm the youngest of four, the only girl."

"That must have been interesting. Any twins in your family?" Paul was thoroughly enjoying this.

"I have a twin brother named Jack. You were the best man at his wedding."

"Not tonight I wasn't."

"You also saved him from drowning when we were in high school." She pointed out the window toward the inky water below. "Not far from here, in fact."

"You must be thinking of someone else," he countered with a wink.

Two could play this game, she decided. "How about you? What's your family like?"

"I have an older sister. She's been married for a couple of years but has yet to produce a grandchild for our overeager mother. I, in turn, broke our father's heart when I decided not to follow him into medicine, but instead to convert the pictures in my head into tangible objects. Like houses and buildings."

"So you're in the construction industry?"

"I'm an architect."

"What a coincidence. I'm in the building industry as well." As much as Moira hated to admit it, she was having fun. "Who do you work for?"

"I own my own firm," he said, maneuvering the SUV around a snowbank and up to the entrance of the restaurant, then throwing it into park. "It's a small, local operation for now, but I'm considering merging with a firm in Portland."

That was news to Moira. Paul had never mentioned what he was doing in Portland.

Just then the valet appeared, suspending the conversation. "Good evening," the young man greeted. "Welcome to Big Water Grille."

"Thank you," Moira responded, taking his gloved hand. Or so she thought. Their hands never clasped and she lost her footing on the slick pavement. Her feet flew out from under her and her tailbone hit the ground with a thud.

"Moira!" Paul came running over. "Are you okay?"

"Yeah," she winced, hand at the small of her back. "Damn high heels. I should have worn my other boots."

Waving off the other man, Paul crouched down beside her. "That'd be two nights in a row. Isn't that a fashion faux pas?"

The fact that he'd noticed astounded, then thrilled Moira. "You remember what boots I wore last night?"

He took her hands in his. "I remember everything about last night," he replied. "Especially—"

Paul was interrupted by a nervous man in a suit and tie. "Ma'am are you okay? Here, let me help you up."

"I have her," Paul told him, pulling Moira up with him.

But Moira had to know what Paul was about to say. "Especially what?"

He gave her a blank look. "What?"

"What were you saying? About last night?"

"Nothing." He shook off whatever he'd been thinking. "But I like these boots better," he told her, squeezing her hand. "They show off your legs. Let's get inside. You must be freezing."

Dumbstruck, she could only nod, letting him lead her into the restaurant.

The alpenglow cast bands of pastel shadows across the charcoal sky as the hostess led them to a table with a panoramic view of Lake Tahoe. After they were seated and the waitress took their drink order, Paul asked, "Now, where were we? Oh, yes. What do you do again?"

Apparently they were back to the first date scenario. "I do the books for my family's business," Moira humored him. "Brody and Sons Construction. Maybe you've heard of us?"

"Of course. I don't call on contractors though." He paused. "Like a…"

Moira threw him a coy look and took the bait. "Window salesman?"

"Exactly. But I know the Brody's excellent reputation."

The waitress returned and divested their wine, courtesy of the lawsuit leery manager. After she left, Paul continued the charade. "So, you're from the area?"

"Born and raised," Moira said as the smooth, earthy vintage slid down her throat, warming her insides. "You?"

"Me too," he mocked coincidence. "Do you get up to the lake often?"

"My friend's family has a place here in Incline Village," she told him, as if he didn't already know. "We came up a lot when we were growing up. Winter and summer."

"Same here. I prefer the summer myself. I'm not much of a skier. Golf's my game. How about you? Do you ski?"

Momentarily flashing back to her first mortifying moment with Jason last night, she answered, "Yes, I grew up skiing with my brothers. I'm a little rusty of late. Life gets in the—"

"Hey, you two."

Moira lifted her high-spirited gaze in the direction of the husky voice over her shoulder. She felt her face start to go slack, but caught it just in time.

"Sarah." Paul's voice was unusually high. He stood in greeting. "Hey, Michelle. It's like a high school reunion here tonight."

"I know," Sarah Worthington agreed eagerly. Her gaze shifted from Paul to Moira and lingered. "Long time no see, Moira. How have you been?"

Moira painted on a smile and returned the perfunctory greeting. "Great," she replied coolly, hoping the over-processed blonde hadn't witnessed her ungainly arrival. "Yourself?"

"Not as well as you apparently. Don't you look fantastic tonight?"

Moira allowed herself a moment to absorb the backhanded compliment before matching its hollow tone. "Likewise." She turned and gave the other woman a more sincere greeting. "Hi, Michelle."

"Hi." Michelle Flynn's gray eyes scanned the room for the second time in thirty seconds. "Is Jack with you guys?" she asked nervously.

Moira put her out of her misery. "No."

"Oh." She let out a relieved breath. "I thought maybe you were all out together."

"Not tonight."

Sarah glanced at the table. "So, it's just the two of you then?" she confirmed unnecessarily.

"Yeah," Paul chimed in. "A belated Valentine's Day dinner."

"How cozy." Sarah's eyes clung to Paul's for a little too long before returning to Moira. "All dressed up, too." She nodded subtly as if mentally connecting the dots and coming to an unexpected conclusion.

Moira couldn't resist. "Galentine's Day dinner for you guys?"

The two women exchanged a nuanced look of discernment. Then Michelle spoke, "Kind of. I'm just starting to get out again after moving back to town. And Sarah's been traveling a lot for work. We needed a night to catch-up."

When Moira only nodded, Sarah put in, "Well, we should get going. It was great to see you both."

"Thanks. You guys too," Paul returned.

"Enjoy your dinner." Sarah's loaded stare vacillated between the two of them, then locked on Moira. "I highly recommend the salmon. The caper sauce was beyond compare. No leftovers for me." She turned on her heel and walked slowly away.

Moria's eyes were still piercing her retreating back when she realized Michelle was talking to her.

"It was so nice to see you, Moira."

Moira turned to her. "You, too."

"Please give Jack," she stopped short and quickly qualified, "I mean your family my best."

The jury in Moira's mind was still out on that. "I will."

She started to walk away, then pulled back, adding, "Maybe we can get together sometime. For lunch or drinks after work." Her tone was cautious, her eyes conflicted.

Truth be told Moira would have liked that, but they both knew it was impossible. "That would be great," she lied.

"I'll give you a call sometime." She directed her final words at Paul. "Bye."

"See ya, Michelle," he responded with a smile, sitting back down.

Suddenly, as if waiting in the wings, the waitress reappeared. "Have we decided on dinner, folks?" she put forth merrily.

Moira stared at the leather-bound menu blankly for a few blinks, then handed it to the waitress. "Surprise me. Anything but the salmon."

*****

"Okay, what's wrong?" Paul asked Moira two hours later. "You hardly touched your dinner."

"Nothing's wrong. I just wasn't hungry." That makes two nights in a row she didn't eat the dinner a man had bought for her. For two completely different reasons. No, she self-corrected, for the same reason.

"This is about running into Sarah and Michelle, isn't it?"

"No."

"Everything was fine before that."

Why did she still let Sarah get to her? Same reason she'd picked at her dinner, Moira reminded herself.

"Michelle was nice," Paul was pointing out.

"She always is. I don't know why she still lets Sarah boss her around. Two decades is surely long enough."

"Why do you and Sarah hate each other again?"

"We don't hate each other," Moira denied inadequately.

Paul grunted. "Had me fooled. Wasn't there some rumor she supposedly spread about you?"

"You mean that I lost my virginity in the seventh grade?"

"That's the one."

"She and Lindsay never got along either. I don't remember why."

58

"That's it?" Paul shifted gears to accommodate their increasing downhill speed. "You were shooting daggers at her with your eyes because of an ancient rumor? And because she and Lindsay never got along?"

"It's been so long, I really don't know why I don't like her. I just don't. And the feeling is clearly mutual. Did you hear that leftover comment?"

Paul took a minute, as if mentally rewinding the conversation. "You mean about her dinner being so good there weren't any leftovers?"

"Yeah."

"So?" They were at the base of Mount Rose now, stopped at a light.

"That was girl code. She wasn't talking about her dinner. She was talking about you."

"Me?" Paul flabbergasted.

"Yeah. First you and Lindsay. Fidgeting in her seat, Moira finished quietly, "Now you and me."

Paul didn't respond and they drove the rest of the way in heavy silence. When they reached her house he paused for a long moment in the driveway, as if collecting his thoughts, before getting out of the car. He opened the passenger door for her with a tight smile and a level stare. Stomach churning with misgiving and disappointment, Moira took his silent direction and stepped out. He shut the door, then took her hand and led them up the driveway, dusted with fresh snow. He punched in the code and she followed him through the garage and into the kitchen, her hand still in his. She owed him an apology and they both knew it. "Paul, I'm sorry," she began, as the garage door ground closed behind them. "I'm sorry I let Sarah get to me. Dinner was lovely and I shouldn't have—" was all she got out.

"It's impossible, isn't it?" Paul scoffed, whirling around to face her. "It's impossible for us to have a first date." Releasing her, he ran an angry hand through his hair and began to pace. "What was I thinking? I know your garage code, for God's sake." He reached over and flipped on the overhead lights. "I know where all the light switches are. Because I drew the fucking kitchen! How many first dates can say that?"

She followed him with her eyes as the trepidation in her stomach turned to panic. "Paul, what's going on? You're scaring me."

"Tell me about it. Do you know what I really remember about last night?"

Moria shook her head in confusion. "*Last* night?"

"Not the boots you were wearing," Paul shot back. "How I felt when I saw you in them. Because you were wearing them for someone else! I've never seen you with another man like that before!"

"I wasn't *with* him!"

"That's not how it looked to me!" He waved a frustrated hand in the air and resumed his rant. "I was up half the night rehashing it in my mind. And I thought tonight you would be that way with me;

your eyes sparkling with anticipation, your step light, your smile jewel-bright."

Was he blind? "I was!"

"Not like that you weren't," he contended with a sad shake of the head. "Because it can never be that way with us. Brand-new like that. We're too..." he searched the kitchen for the word, then finished, "familiar."

"And that's bad?" she baffled, slapping the sides of her thighs.

"I wanted tonight to be special, romantic, different. I wanted to woo you."

"You did," she said, going to him. "It was. I'm the one who let the past get in the way."

"I think I've been letting the past get in the way for a lot longer than tonight." He let out a deliberate breath, then put his arms around her and held her eyes in his. "Moira, something is happening between us."

She smiled up at him. "Well, that's new. So maybe we just have to amend our first date expectations a little. I promise to try if you will."

"Moira..." He brushed his lips over hers in silent agreement. She sensed him start to pull away, but his mouth lingered and began moving over hers, gently at first and then more ardently, purposefully. Her arms circled his neck, bringing him to her, yielding to the pent-up need, to the joy of being in his arms again. He nudged her lips apart and his tongue began flirting with hers, inching in and out of her mouth, around her lips, giving and taking as she fell deeper and deeper into each kiss, into him, in love.

His mouth left hers on choppy, reluctant breaths. His tongue skated down her neck and she tipped her head back, surrendering to the rapturous sensations and newfound want swirling inside her. He made a silky path to her earlobe, nibbling on it before returning to her mouth. Her hands were in his hair now and his entire mouth was covering hers, as if his couldn't be satiated no matter how unsparingly he kissed her. His hands roved up and down her back, finally encompassing her waist, pressing her so tightly against him it was hard to know where she left off and he began. Mumbling her name, he tore his mouth away from hers and buried his face in her hair. They stood there, holding each other and heaving shallow breaths, striving for calm while their heartbeats soared and their pulses pounded. Finally, Paul croaked, "I had to stop. I don't trust myself. I should go."

"I trust you. And I don't want you to go," Moira heard herself say.

He pulled out of her embrace just enough to meet her eyes. His were full of want and need and laced with something else Moira had never seen in them before. He cradled her face in his hands. "Are you sure? Because there's no going back then. To the way we were."

"I don't want to go back to the way we were. Do you?"

"No. But I can't lose you either."

"Why would you lose me?"

"Because there's no in-between here, no gray area, no friends with benefits bullshit for us. Moira, do you know what this means? What we're all but saying?"

She could do nothing but nod at him, as her heart swelled in her chest and her throat threatened to close.

"God, I'm such an idiot. I've wasted so much time."

"Me too. Let's not waste anymore."

He laid his lips softly on hers, then said, "We need to straighten something out first. About tonight. I don't care what Sarah was really talking about. Or what she thinks. Or what she thinks she knows. All I care about is what you think, what you know. Is that how you feel? That I'm the leftovers? Or worse yet, that you are?"

"Of course not," she told him. "Well, maybe a little," she qualified with a self-deprecating grimace. "Me, I mean."

"Don't. That couldn't be further from the truth." He huffed out a breath and finished with care, "Lindsay and I never slept together, if that's where Sarah was going with that."

"I know."

Humor flashed into his eyes. "Of course you do. You guys probably have a full dossier on each other."

Moira ignored the comment; they both knew she couldn't deny it. "I need to know something too."

He rubbed her shoulders. "Yeah."

"I need to make sure you don't want me just because someone else does," she said, suddenly terrified.

That seemed to throw him, like he had to take a moment, dig deep for the answer. Moira could feel her heart beating outside of her chest, her stomach doing somersaults, her hands begin to shake around his waist. Finally, he answered in a quiet voice, "I do want you because someone else does. And I would still want you even if no one else did. But most of all, I want you because I love you, Moira. I think I really love you."

CHAPTER EIGHT

Paul watched as surprise and joy rolled slowly across Moira's face. Then her eyes began to glisten and she whispered, "You do?"

"I still can't believe it, but I do," he told her incredulously. "Maybe I always have."

She sucked in air, let it out through bated breath and professed, "I love you, too. I have for a while."

Relief washing over him, he raised a grateful hand to her cheek. "But you never said anything, acted any differently."

"What else could I do?" she bargained through a shrug. "My two best friends were marrying each other. I couldn't mess that up. I figured it was just some passing fancy."

"But it wasn't," he confirmed carefully.

Moira pressed her lips together and shook her head from side to side.

"Do you want it to be?"

"Not anymore." Her voice was tentative. "Not if you feel the same way."

Paul could feel her eyes on his back as he stepped away and walked to the window, absently taking in the backyard. The snow was starting to accumulate and all was dark but for the light of the moon battling the low, heavy clouds for prominence. He likened it to the war being fought in his gut, one of elation and panic. "That's the scariest thing I've ever heard."

"It is?" Moira bewildered.

"Yeah." He spun around to face her. "Because there's definitely no going back now."

"Why would I want to go back to a one-sided love affair?" Her voice trailed off as the possibility took hold. She took a marked step backward, as if shielding herself from his words with distance. "Oh."

"I don't want to go back either!" Reaching her in three quick strides, he clarified, "I mean it's all or nothing for me."

She gave him a shy smile. "I'm all in if you are."

"Moira…" Paul wrapped her in his arms. He simply could not let go of her. He wondered if he'd ever want to again. He felt her racing heart settle, her breathing relax, then fall into rhythm with his. And that indescribable feeling come over him again. Then as if suddenly struck by some metamorphic force, he realized what it had been all along. Love. It was true love. It was Moira. She was the one. She'd always been the one. He'd just been too blind or too stubborn to too scared to let himself see it, feel it, accept it. But he banked that realization for now and said, "I can't believe I told you like that. Standing in the kitchen."

"Then why don't you tell me again? Somewhere else?"

Pangs of yearning flooding his body, Paul leaned out of her embrace. "I want to do more than tell you. I want to show you."

The weight his words hung in the air between them for a few silent beats. Then she linked her arms behind his neck and said in a round, smoky voice, "You know the way."

He laid a long, affecting kiss on her lips. She tilted her head back, allowing him to plant rows of kisses up and down her neck. He felt the low growl in her throat, the contented moan of her mouth, the acquiescence of her body as he picked her up and carried her through the shadowed hallway. The bedroom was washed in snowy light and smelled like her perfume melded with fresh linen. He put her down next to the bed and traced her lips with his fingers, then skirted them over her chest. All his blood was rushing to his cock now, taking his moral compass with it. He had to concentrate on stopping himself from hurling the dress over her head, throwing her down on the bed and taking her. But he couldn't. Because she was Moira. And he wanted their first time to be better than that. He brushed the stray tendrils away from her face. "I can't believe this is happening," he told her with hushed reverence.

She was looking at him through dewy, amorous eyes weaved with uneasiness. His hard-on wanted ignore the latter, but his conscience wouldn't let him. "Are you sure about this?"

She answered by taking his mouth in a long, slow kiss, then laying her head on his shoulder. "I've never been more sure about anything."

"Then what is it?" he muttered in her ear. Her arms slid down his back to circle his waist and she was holding him so tightly against her that she could no doubt tell how sure he was.

"Paul," she began in a shaky voice. "It's my first time."

*****

As nervous as she was, Moira had to laugh a little inside. At that moment she could have knocked Paul over with a feather.

His entire body went ramrod straight and he took a measured step backward, out of her arms. He deadpanned her, eyes wide and mouth agape for a full ten seconds. Finally, he astounded, "It is? Moira, my God."

"I know it seems unimaginable," she started with a resigned sigh. "But there hasn't been anyone that special in my life."

Paul took a stunned hand to his forehead. His expression bordering on panicked, he managed, "I can't believe it."

"It is a little embarrassing. Considering my age."

"I think it's wonderful." He returned to her and cradled her face in his hands. "I'm honored."

That's what Moira had been afraid of. "I don't want that," she told him in no uncertain terms. "I want you to treat me like you would any other woman."

"That's impossible." Paul took exception with a decisive shake of the head. "You're not any other woman. You're Moira."

"Exactly. And if I were anyone else, you'd be making love to me by now, right?"

Dropping his hands to his sides, he looked away as if the chair in the corner held the answer. "I couldn't have done that anyway. You could never be like any other woman."

She brought his gaze back to hers with a finger to his chin. "I can be, if you let me. You said it yourself. We can't go back."

"This is different."

"You're right," she challenged, sounding more confident than she felt inside. "What if I disappoint you?"

His eyes fired with indignation. "You could never disappoint me." He kissed her long and hard as if to prove it. "See, there they go again."

Moira cocked her head to one side and furrowed her brow in confusion.

"The fireworks," he clarified. "They seem to go off in my gut every time I kiss you. Making love to you might burn me up from the inside out." Then his expression lighted. "But I'm willing to risk it."

"At least I'm not the only one. But I've never been in love before, so I wouldn't know."

That seemed to unnerve him a little, give him pause, that she felt it too. Finally, he said, "Maybe you have. Maybe we've been in love with each other for half our lives without realizing it."

"But what about—"

Paul silenced her protesting lips with his, then told her, "That doesn't even begin to compare. How long have you felt this way?"

"I honestly don't know. I still can't decide if it happened overnight or changed gradually over time. I just know that when you look into my eyes my stomach jumps and my pulse races. And sometimes I can't seem to get you out of my mind."

"And seeing me with Lindsay didn't bother you?"

"It did," she admitted solemnly. "Did it bother you knowing that deep down she was still in love with Brian?"

"Not like seeing you with Window Man last night did." Paul's face became a dark, disgusted frown. "I wanted to strangle that guy with my bare hands. And when you said he kissed you." He finished through clenched teeth, "I felt steam coming out of my ears. I wanted to scrub him off your lips."

Moira wondered if her cheeks were betraying her as the inner delight spread from head to toe. "And now?"

"Now I want to do something very different to your lips." His body moved into hers and he covered her mouth with his again. And all the books she'd read, all the movies she'd seen, all the scenarios she'd created in her head couldn't have prepared her for what Paul said next. "Pack a bag."

CHAPTER NINE

"Nothing?" Paul was saying into his phone, blazing a trail across Moira's bedroom floor. "I know, I know," he dismayed, raking his free hand through his hair. She had obliged him by getting an overnight bag together. Now twenty minutes later, she was quite sure no woman ever had so much foreknowledge and to-do ahead of losing her virginity.

Paul disconnected and met her expectant gaze. "No rooms. Valentine's Day weekend."

"Why do we need a room again?"

"We're going to do this right."

"I wouldn't know otherwise. Besides, we have a perfectly good room here." She gestured in the air with the palm of her outstretched hand. "Three of them to be exact."

He came to her. "I want it to be special for you."

She cuffed his wrists. "What could be more special than making love in the house we remodeled together? In the room you helped me paint? In the bed we moved around a hundred times until we got it just right?"

He processed that through a cleansing breath. Then he kissed her so tenderly that she swore her heart would burst into a million tiny pieces inside her chest. "Moira," he murmured, "why did it take me so long to realize that I'm madly in love with you?"

She saw the raw emotion in his eyes and matched it in her tone. "Why did it take me so long to realize that I've been saving myself for you? Don't make me wait any longer."

His hands slid down to her hips, pausing before scooping her up and straddling her to his middle. She wrapped her legs around him, catching a fleeting glimpse of herself in the mirror as Paul turned them toward the bed. Even in the soft light she looked like a hot mess. Her hair was disheveled and not in a sexy bedroom way and the smudged liner rimmed her eyes in a gratuitous, walk of shame way. She wondered who she would see the next time she looked in the mirror. Not a virgin, that was for sure.

Paul laid her down on the bed, and standing above her, got out of his blazer and unbuttoned his shirt. She'd seen him shirtless before; they'd spent many summer days up at the lake. But it was as if she was seeing him for the first time. His pecs were defined but not too muscular; his ab muscles developed just enough to form a natural-looking six-pack; his upper arms strong and toned. She could feel her heart leap in her chest and desire begin to build inside her as he lowered himself down on the bed next to her. He turned her toward him and gathered her in his arms. "I've wanted you for so long without even knowing it," he amazed. "Like I've never wanted anybody before."

Moira gulped. "Then take me."

"I'll go easy. I promise."

"I'm not going to break."

His eyes fired with lust. "Be careful what you wish for."

She responded by reaching under her dress at the shoulder and shimmying it down to just above her breast, then doing the same with the other side. Rolling on her back, she got out of the sleeves, shuffling the bodice down to her hips. She turned back to him and immediately commended herself for buying a new black bra as lascivious appreciation filled his eyes.

"You are so beautiful. I can't wait to see the rest of you." He lavished her mouth with long, deep, lazy kisses before his fingertips grazed her throat and chest as if searching for a place to start. He settled on the swell of her breasts, then began making tiny circles on her nipples through the lace of the bra before removing it and tossing it aside. He took in her breasts for a moment, indulging in them with his eyes, before taking one in each hand. "Even sexier than I imagined."

Moira was just as turned on by the admission as by his caress. "You've thought about me naked? How I'd look?"

"Oh, yeah. Lately it's all I can think about."

Moira laid her hands on top of his. "Show me."

"My pleasure." Ranging himself on top of her with her legs between his, he took one breast in his mouth while he brought the other to point with his thumb. Nibble by nibble, he tugged, sucked, licked. She held his head against her, wanting him take more of her in his mouth, as the pull in her stomach crept downward and she began to arch beneath him. She muttered his name and he returned to her mouth as if he'd been long-starved of it, of her, of this coupling. She surrendered to him completely then; her mouth, her body, her heart. And soon, she knew, the most delicate part of her.

She loved feeling his weight on her. And with it, even through his pants, his burgeoning erection. She felt a shiver of want run down her spine, a rash of heat flash through her body as his mouth left hers and showered her chest and stomach with kisses, pausing just above where the dress rested. He lifted his head and met her gaze, as if asking for permission to go farther. She granted it by grasping each side of the bunched-up dress and wiggling it down her legs, then kicking it and her boots onto the floor.

The look on Paul's face was one of wanton gratefulness instead of lascivious appreciation when he saw the matching panties. The lace triangle barely covered the vee between her thighs and was attached to thin strings that rested on her hip bones. Crawling back to her, he cupped her bare buttocks. "I want to touch every inch of you. I love having my hands on you," he gushed. "All of you fits perfectly in them."

"I've never bought a thong before," she told him throatily. "There's not much to it. Do you like it?"

"Oh, I like it all right. But I'd like it better on the floor." He made quick work of his pants, then eased the thong down in short order. He paused for a few seconds, tasting her with his eyes. Then he laid on his side next to her and placed a hand on her center. "I don't want to rush you, but I can't wait much longer to make love to you."

Despite the bundle of nerves juxtaposing the ribbon of desire swirling in her stomach, she got out, "Tell me what to do."

"You'll know." He guided her hand to him. He was hard and seeping inside the black briefs. She began to stroke him, slowly at first and then more firmly, hungrily. His breath caught in his throat and his eyes rolled back in his head, then closed carnally. She wondered if he could grow any more aroused without bursting in her hand. The tip of him was oozing now and she likened it to the hedonic wicking between her legs. Just then he reached for her and felt it for himself. "Oh God," he moaned. "You're dripping." In one smooth move, he kicked off the briefs and rolled on top of her. His erection rested against her pelvis and he brushed his lips across hers. "Now. I need to be inside you now."

Bracing herself, she answered the hint of prayer in his voice by spreading her thighs in silent invitation. She felt his hand between her legs, then his hardness find her. She winced a bit when he began inching into her.

"It's going to hurt a little," he warned gently.

"I know."

"I'll go slow." He slid the palms of his hands up her back and crushed her breasts against his chest as he entered her. His eyes, solicitous now, found hers. "I love you, Moira."

"I love you, too."

"Oh, baby," he cried out in a low growl, filling her. "You're so wet, so tight, so soft."

She wondered if he could also feel the fever that was sweeping through her. Or the barrier of resistance shattering in its wake. Her hips began to sway with his, each thrust bringing less sting and more yearning. Rising on his haunches, he positioned himself between her raised legs and drove himself deeper into her, rocking them faster and faster, nearly flying above her. He was tapping the very essence of her now, teasing her with climax. She felt aglow, like all the energy in her body had dovetailed into a cluster of spasms between her thighs.

"Put your legs around my neck," he begged through thready moans.

She obliged just as his entire body tensed. Her name escaped his lips as waves of heat began to overtake her, free her, and he exploded into her.

CHAPTER TEN

He should be shot on the spot.

And kicked.

And left for dead.

He'd been level out of the gate, but once he was inside her, the shameless animal in him took over and chased away every ounce of decency he had. And it was yet to return because all he could think about was doing it again. Disgusted with himself, he kept his head buried in her hair, too contrite to face her. Until from somewhere in the darkness came his name. He pulled back and found her gazing up at him with bright eyes and a dreamy smile. Maybe he wasn't such a deplorable ass after all. "Yeah." He kissed her softly. "You okay?"

Moira contemplated that for longer than Paul would have liked. Then she affirmed with a weak nod.

He feathered her cheek with the backs of his fingers and was shifting his weight to one side when he felt something on her legs. He turned on the bedside lamp, then sprang back in alarm. Ruddy-colored spots covered her thighs and the sheet below. "No, you're not! You're bleeding!"

"I know. I'm sorry."

"Sorry?" Paul was appalled. "Why are *you* sorry?" He ran a panicked hand through his hair.

"*I'm* the one who should be sorry. Look at what I've done to you!"

She gave him a reassuring look. "You didn't do anything to me that I didn't want done. That's what happens the first time."

Despite making sense, that didn't sit well with him, make him feel any less responsible. "What can I do?" he entreated. "What can I get you?"

She took a moment, then began is a hesitant voice, "I know I should get cleaned up. I don't want to gross you out. But I loved laying with you. I loved the way you were holding me."

Paul was blown away. Even after what he'd done to her, she still wanted him. Grabbing the blanket from the end of the bed, he laid back down and spread it over them. He gathered her in his arms and brought her against him. She rested her head on his chest. "I love being like this with you, too." Except it was making him grow again. He wondered if she noticed.

"I'm so glad it was you. I can't imagine being with someone I didn't really know. Someone I didn't love."

He found himself hoping she never would. And that shook him to the very core. "It gets better," he told her. "I promise."

"Will you show me?"

"Mold you into my own little sex fiend?" he joked. "Absolutely."

Her head still on his chest, she shot him a serious look. "I want you to want me."

"I do." In a way he'd never wanted a woman before. But he didn't want to scare her, rush her, so he kept that to himself. Laying a kiss on the top of her head, he rubbed his hand up and down her back and held her close.

They laid there in silence for a few minutes until Moira said, "I really should get cleaned up."

She started to sit up, but he pulled her back down. He turned her to face him, and looked deeply into her eyes. She was so beautiful, so genuine, so vulnerable. He clasped her face in his hands and kissed her, giving into all the emotions churning inside him. Then he brought her back into his arms. "Not quite yet. This is a first for me too, you know."

"Oh?" she replied in a tone laced with humor. "How so?"

"I've never slept with someone on the first date." Or found myself in love with them, he silently added.

"Well, I guess that makes us even," she agreed facetiously.

He tipped her chin up to meet his gaze again. "I'm glad it was me too."

She let the words register, then gave him an endearing smile and a peck on the lips. "I'll be right back."

Paul reflected on her retreating back, reprimanding himself again for taking her innocence to task as the sound of rushing water filled the air. He had to do something to make this right. He threw on his pants and stripped the bed, then headed for the laundry room. He put the sheets in the washer and made his way to the kitchen. The lights were still blazing and he grabbed a mug and surveyed the drawer under the coffee maker. There were precious few tea choices among the dark roasts, so green tea would have to do. He started the machine and found himself staring at it mindlessly as it sputtered and steamed. Raking a restless hand through his hair, he tried to get a grip on himself. He'd only just had her and all he could think about was having her again. Even more of her this time. He was beyond reproach, a complete and total ass, so he had only one choice. He had to get out of there.

Moira liked half and half in her coffee, so tea would probably follow suit. He doctored the tea and made it back to the bedroom just as she was emerging from the bathroom. She was wrapped in a towel and her hair was twisted loosely into a clip at the top of her head. Paul felt himself begin to grow again, thinking about what was under that towel. And as much as he loved her long curls, her bare neck looked incredibly sexy. He would start there, then make his way down her throat to her breasts. He'd loved how she'd squirmed beneath him when he'd taken one, then the other, in his mouth. He'd leave them and lick his way down to her stomach. And the thought of his mouth going farther sent a shiver of lust through his body so erotic that he felt himself begin to ooze.

"What's this?" Moira was asking.

He shook off the fantasy. "Tea. I thought it would help you sleep." He set the mug on the nightstand.

"Thanks. No tea for you?" she asked, her expectant smile giving way to a confused frown.

"I won't have any trouble sleeping." He sent her a devilish grin.

She ignored his attempt at humor and took in the room. "You stripped the bed."

"Yeah. But I didn't want to interrupt you in the bathroom to get to the linen closet for sheets." And I was afraid I wouldn't have been able to keep my hands off of you, he reminded himself.

"It wouldn't have been an interruption."

"I can make up the bed while you get dressed," he offered gamely.

"Okay," she returned warily.

He stuck his hands in his pockets for safekeeping as he walked past her and into the bathroom. He grabbed the first set of sheets he saw. "These okay?" His voice was suddenly unreliable.

"Sure," she replied, still standing at the threshold of the door.

"Why aren't you getting dressed?"

"Paul, what's wrong?" she asked evenly.

"Nothing." He could feel her eyes on him as he unfolded the sheets on the bed. "Are you busy tomorrow?"

"Tomorrow?" she repeated unnecessarily. "No, I guess not."

"I'll call you in the morning then." He wondered if she heard the struggle in his voice. Or could sense his heart racing. Or see his cock getting harder. He tried to busy himself, securing one corner of the bottom sheet, then another. When she didn't respond, he looked up.

She was standing there, still in her towel, staring at him, dumbfounded.

He cleared his throat. "Okay?"

"Okay," she answered with a catch in her voice.

Who was he kidding? He didn't want to leave any more than she wanted him to. He simply could not stop himself from going to her. He took her hands in his, fighting the urge to take her in his arms. "I don't want to go but I have to," he attempted to explain. "You need to heal."

She was biting her bottom lip and her eyes were beginning to fill.

"If I stay I won't be able to keep my hands off of you!" He grasped her hands tighter. "Do you understand?"

She made a catlike sound from deep in her throat and shook her head affirmatively.

His pleading gaze met her watery one head-on. "I won't be able to stop myself from taking you again! Even harder!"

"I don't want you to stop yourself," she stated quietly. "You said it gets better. Prove it."

*****

"You sure you're up to it?" Paul was half-heartedly asking. "I can stay and try to keep my hands to myself."

She was sore; actually she felt like she'd been torn in two. But she would keep that to herself. Because if the sweeping pleasure that had started building before was any indication of what was to come, some passing discomfort was well worth it. And she'd never felt so loved, so wanted, so needed as she had when he climaxed. He'd been so sweet, so gentle, right up to the end. Then he'd started to come unhinged. And that had been the best part. She gave him a roguish smile. "I'm fine. But if you're not up for another round..."

With that, Paul picked her up and carried her to the half-made bed. "Now you've done it." He set her down and laid on top of her. "Are you going to show me what's under that towel?"

"Aren't you the one who wanted me to get dressed?"

"I didn't *want* you to get dressed. It was the only chance I had of leaving you alone."

"It wouldn't have worked. I don't want you to leave me alone."

"What do you want?"

She answered by unzipping his pants, then pushing them down just past his hips. He finished the job from there, and as he met her eyes again she untucked the towel, holding his stare as she opened it. It hadn't been half an hour since he'd seen her naked, but he studied her as if it was the first time, as if he was memorizing every inch of her. She felt an anticipatory quiver run through her as he slid an arm underneath her and pressed her naked body to his. He was already erect and that made the quiver become an eager ache between her thighs. He crushed his mouth down on hers, kissing her with matching conviction.

"Don't hold back this time," she told him when his mouth left hers.

"I won't," he panted, as his hands made their way down her sides. "I can't."

His hand rested just below her stomach and she felt a twinge deep inside her. But that was nothing compared to the swooning she felt when his fingers found her. "Oh, Paul. Oh, God."

"Let go. Let me take you there." He fondled her folds, stirring a craving in her like she'd never known. She heard him moan in appreciation as his fingers dipped inside her, one and then two, darting in and out, increasing in speed and depth. She wanted to reach for him, bring him with her, but something was surging inside her, taking hold of her. She could feel herself starting to unravel, as waves of pleasure flooded every cell in her body, stealing her breath and drenching him in her tracks. She climaxed, wondering how she'd gone this long without this release, without this connection, without him.

Paul muttered words of gratitude as he entered her. She raised her hips in welcome, feeling herself tighten around him. His eyes, rushing like a runaway river, met hers and he began to move inside her. She bent her knees, letting him penetrate her deeper, bear down even harder. And just as she felt herself begin to crest again, he groaned her name and unleashed himself into her.

CHAPTER ELEVEN

A few hours later, Paul awoke to an indistinct screeching.

"Moira!"

The voice was familiar. Too familiar. And it immediately tore him out of his lovemaking-induced sleep. "Shit," he mumbled under his breath. He opened his eyes and got his bearings. He was waking up in Moira's room, in Moira's bed, in Moira's arms. To the sound of another man's voice.

"Moira? You decent?"

Paul swore again and brought a resigned hand to his forehead. Spending the night was one thing. Waking up to the brother of the woman you spent the night with was another. Especially when that brother was Jack Brody. And most especially when the woman was Moira, sleeping naked against him, with the curve of her breast peeking out from beneath the sheet and her hair strewn across the pillow they'd all but shared. With whom he was decidedly and utterly in love, Paul reminded himself with terrified amazement. And remarkably, she felt the same way. He was still mulling that over when she began to stir beside him. After a few throaty grunts and drowsy blinks, her eyes fluttered open. He watched a mischievous smile spread across her face.

"Good morning."

"It certainly is." He could feel the desire start to build in him again, like an itch that could never be completely scratched. Sliding a leg between her slightly parted ones, he rolled on top of her and skimmed his lips over hers. "I was just thinking." He started nibbling her neck. "That was the best first date ever."

She tipped her head back and he felt the giggle rise in her throat before she released it and looped her arms around his neck. "It sure was."

His mouth was making its way back to hers when Jack's resounding voice filled the air again. "Coffee's ready!"

Moria froze, then jerked her head forward in alarm.

"By the way, Jack's in the kitchen," Paul informed her easily.

"Oh." She gulped. "Why?"

"Good question. How about I go find out while you get dressed? We can pick up where we left off later." There was no getting around dealing with this; it was bound to happen eventually.

"Go get 'em tiger."

"Very funny." He left a fleeting kiss on her lips before donning his pants and heading for the kitchen. He found Jack standing in front of the window over the sink staring out at the backyard.

"Coffee?" he offered without turning around.

"I'll get it." Paul grabbed two mugs.

"I came over to blow the driveway," Jack explained as if to justify his presence. "We got dumped on last night."

"I can blow the driveway."

"I didn't expect you to be here."

"You and me both. But I am, aren't I?"

"Yes, you are."

"Get used to it. This was the first time, but it won't be the last."

With a tight nod, Jack turned to face to him. He had strawberry blonde hair to Moira's raven black and right now it was covered by a Patagonia beanie, giving his high forehead prominence. "I'm not sure how I feel about that."

"You should feel fine about it. It was your idea."

"It was Emily's idea," he corrected sharply.

Holding Jack's steely gaze over the top of the coffee cup, Paul took a sip. "So are you okay with it?"

"Does it matter?"

Paul snickered. "Not really."

"Then you must care about her. So I'm okay with it."

"I love her," Paul informed him.

Jack seemed unimpressed. "You've been there before, haven't you?"

"Hadn't you?"

That threw him a bit but he recovered quickly. "Touché."

"Sorry," Paul said and meant it. "That was low."

Jack accepted the apology, tipping his head imperceptibly as men do.

"Speaking of which, we saw Michelle last night."

Jack's deep-set eyes narrowed. "I heard she was back in town."

"She looked good."

"I didn't ask how she looked, did I?"

"No, you didn't." Paul cut his friend some slack. "She asked about you, though."

Jack chewed on that for a few seconds. Then he drained his coffee mug and set it in the sink. "I'm going out to blow the driveway."

Confident he'd made his position clear, Paul offered, "We can knock it out together in no time. Do you still have work boots in the garage?"

"I'll do the driveway. You have your hands full."

"At least we can agree on that," Paul replied in good humor.

Jack started to walk away, but turned on his heel and allowed, "She loves you too, according to my wife."

"So I'm told."

"Just don't forget that she's my sister. Treat her as such." So saying, Jack took his leave.

Nodding to himself, Paul contemplated his friend's back for a few seconds. When he turned around, Moira was standing there in a thick robe, still managing to look sexy as hell.

"What was that all about?"

"Your brother is digging you out. He came in for coffee."

Moira crossed her arms over her chest and squinted skeptically. "The man carries a coffee thermos with him at all times." She walked over to Paul and accepted the steaming mug from his hand. "He didn't come in for coffee."

"No, he didn't. He realized it was my car buried in the driveway."

"And what did he think about your car being in my driveway on a Sunday morning?"

"He didn't like it. He's afraid I'm going to hurt you."

She considered that around a long sip. "Are you?"

"I don't know." Paul pulled her to him. "Are you going to hurt me?"

"I hope not."

"I don't."

Her expression fell a little and she cocked her head in confusion.

"We always hurt the people we love the most," he explained with care.

"Then maybe I will," she replied thoughtfully.

"I'm going to hold you to that," Paul said, sealing the deal with a kiss.

CHAPTER TWELVE

"What a bitch."

"I know," Moira agreed the next day without looking up from the computer screen. "She needs to get a life and get over high school."

"And..." Lindsay correctly presumed there was more.

Moira swore under her breath. Sometimes their connection bordered on frightening. "It's probably my imagination, but there was something about the way Sarah looked at Paul. It was like they were speaking in code. She was practically tasting him with her eyes."

Moira heard a drawer shut on the other end of the line and pictured Lindsay, phone stuck into the crook of her shoulder and stomach protruding out in front of her, stocking the nursery dresser. "That's odd," she responded after a long moment. "You'd think she'd consider Paul beneath her. She always went for the boy toy with nothing upstairs or the rich guy with the sports car."

Lindsay was right, yet something told Moira that Paul was the exception to the rule.

"But Sarah is one to want what somebody else has just because they have it," Lindsay was still talking. "Especially something you have."

Moira felt a wide smile replace the horizontal line of concentration across her mouth. She'd never had somebody to call her own before. "Likewise. Keep Brian away from her."

"He'd see right through her," Lindsay stated proudly. "She's as shallow as the lake is deep." She muttered something about socks, then asked, "How's the snowpack up there?"

"It has to be solid. We got nearly a foot down here yesterday. There's probably three feet of fresh powder on the mountain." That reminded Moira of another matter. "What do I do about Jason?" She shifted her gaze to the roses. She still had to deal with his friend request.

"Tell him the truth. You're seeing someone."

"And three days ago I wasn't?"

"You were confused, on a break. Now you've worked it out."

"Doesn't that sound lame? It's not like I'm never going to see him again. He calls on us."

"You kissed him good night, not slept with him." Lindsay paused, then finished with a snort, "Offer to set him up with Sarah."

Moira laughed in spite of herself. "He's too good for her."

"Michelle, then."

"Now that has legs," Moira replied, only half-joking.

"Did you tell Jack you saw her?"

"Paul did."

"How'd he take it?"

"He shut down. As usual."

"Can't blame him. Eight years together and she runs off to Vegas and gets married."

"She didn't run off to Vegas and get married," Moira was quick to refute. "She got caught up, infatuated with a colleague. Probably due to the fact that she'd never dated anyone but my brother. And they actually were on a break. "

"Why are you defending her?"

Why was she? But Moira only said, "You should've seen her, Linds. She was like a deer in headlights when she saw us, thinking Jack was there. We all make mistakes."

"Don't I know it." Lindsay's voice was soft and full of emotion. "All this time Paul was in love with you. And I was standing in the way."

"That's completely different. You didn't know. And neither one of us was ready to see it, let alone admit it."

"Speaking of which, how are you feeling today?" Lindsay wanted to know, her tone rich in innuendo.

Moira felt her checks begin to burn. "Better."

"Paul being out of town this week will give you the time you need to heal. You'll be ready to go at it again in a few days."

Moira was ready now. She already missed him. "I'll take your word for it. Actually, my tailbone is bothering me more than anything. But enough about me. How's baby Grace this morning?"

"The *baby*," Lindsay accentuated, "is very active right now. And stop calling it Grace."

"You're just afraid I'll jinx it."

Lindsay didn't deny that. "I still don't know why you're so sure it's a girl in the first place."

"Fate," Moira told her easily.

There was a meditative lull, then Lindsay said, "I'm almost starting to believe in all this fate stuff you so readily espouse."

"Fate puts us where we're supposed to be."

"And to think," Lindsay pointed out, "you've been there all along."

*****

"That's not what we agreed on, Will."

"Not in certain terms, perhaps. But you knew it was a strong possibility down the road."

"The plan was to horizontally integrate the two companies with independently functioning offices in Reno and Portland," Paul pointed out as diplomatically as possible.

Forming a steeple with his fingers, William Pickett unfolded his rawboned body in the imposing leather chair. "For the time being, yes," he allowed. "But I'm not getting any younger. Pickett Architectural Engineering and Design has a time-honored reputation in Portland. Pickett-Webster Architectural Engineering and Design should be headquartered here as well. You can't earn the respect of my people, let alone the community, from Reno. Modern technology or not."

"That sounds more like an acquisition than a merger."

Pickett was quiet for a long moment, so long that Paul almost spoke. Finally, he said, "There's no denying that you have built a solid, successful company in a relatively short amount of time. But keep in mind that I've been in this business three times longer than you have. I built this place from the ground up with my wife as my only employee for the first three years. Missed a lot of milestones during my daughters' formative years. And yet I find myself in the unlikely position of not having an heir interested in the taking over the fruits of my labors. I'm looking for a partner who would eventually transition to an owner, a successor. If that were to come to fruition, once the new company is firmly established, you could be based in Reno; the call would be yours. But for now, while I'm still working in the business, while we're integrating and aligning things, your unwillingness to relocate to Portland is a potential deal-breaker. I've admired your work from my travels to Nevada and California, which is what prompted me to contact you in the first place. I think we've built a trustworthy professional relationship over the last year. Relocation on your part was at the very least implied from the beginning. I'm sorry if I didn't make that more clear." He ended on a tone of finality, as if the matter had been settled.

Paul sat up a little straighter in the chair facing Pickett's desk, wishing he'd had a better night's sleep. He'd stayed at Moira's again last night and had gotten up at the crack of dawn to go home and pack before catching an early flight to Portland. But he didn't need a clearer head to know that everything the other man was saying made perfect sense. Or he knew that before he let himself fall in love with Moira. "Agreed. And I knew I'd be here more than there at first, but permanently relocating was never part of the deal in my mind," he replied evenly.

The older man stared at Paul solemnly over his cheaters. "Reno was always going to be an auxiliary office, perhaps the first of several in the West. I thought we had an understanding."

"We do," Paul assured him, clearing his throat and meeting the rheumy eyes fixed on him. "But I never formally agreed to pick up my life and move it to Portland. We could be talking about a minimum of five to ten years here."

Pickett's mouth tightened. "This is a sweet deal for you, Paul. The kind of deal I'd offer to a son, a nephew. With your business acumen, my reputation, hard work and a little luck, you could be a rich man by fifty. Retire a hell of a lot younger than me." His gaze shifted to the woman's picture on the credenza and he finished in a voice weaved in ache, "Before it's too late."

Paul gave him an empathetic, tight-mouthed smile. "I appreciate that, I really do. But I considered my weekly presence here long-term, yet temporary. Until the deal is finalized and I became familiar with your operating procedures, your employees, the area. During that time we would hire a manager, likely from within, to act as an intermediary. Someone to fill in the gaps, be hands-on and allow you to transition out of the business over time. I would split my time between the two offices."

"With a five-hundred mile commute?"

"I'd maintain an as needed presence at each office." Paul felt himself losing ground. "Like we outlined in the initial business plan."

Pickett shook his head from side to side. "That was last year. Before all the environmental and earthquake codes were tightened. That, and the changing demographic of this area, is a game-changer. We could have more work in the Pacific Northwest in the next decade than we know what to do with. Portland is an ideal central location. And the new, young blood you would bring to the table would only further that. "

He was right and Paul knew it. "Duly noted. But there are a myriad of parallel opportunities in Reno to grow business as well. Building is booming on both the residential and commercial fronts. And don't forget about Tahoe. The new codes will impact the Southwest and Northern Nevada as well."

Pickett narrowed his eyes, inclined his head to one side and pursed his lips. "What's really going on here, Paul? One of the things that attracted me to your firm was the young, ambitious, open-minded entrepreneur at the helm. Have you been approached by someone else?"

"No, of course not," Paul answered honestly. "I just can't commit to relocating to Portland right now. It would be disingenuous of me."

"Sleep on it for a couple of nights. There's a lot here for a single guy like you. Too many microbreweries to count, artisan coffee, year-round outdoor activities. Hell, you might meet a nice Portland girl and never want to leave."

There was a time when Paul would have jumped at the chance. But now his heart raced and stomach churned at the mere thought. His girl would never be a Portland girl. And that, he shocked himself by thinking, was the ultimate deal-breaker. Reeling himself in, he reiterated, "Let me remind you this would be a merger, not an acquisition."

"It's neither." Pickett tipped his head slightly forward and continued in a hardened voice, "It's a partnership. Properly defined, a partnership is an alliance created to achieve a common goal, a joining of rights and responsibilities, a marriage of sorts. I thought our goal was the same."

"It is."

"Good." He pushed up from behind the desk, signaling the end of the conversation. "Then you'll have to excuse me. I'm expecting a call."

Taking the cue to leave, Paul stood and extended his hand. The two men were exchanging parting pleasantries at the door when Pickett nonchalantly added, "Another fun fact about Portland. It's the perfect climate for growing roses. It's known as the City of Roses."

No, Paul told himself as he walked to the elevator. His girl would never be a Portland girl.

CHAPTER THIRTEEN

"You're in early."

"You know what Dad says about hump day," Jack responded dryly from his desk, looking up from his phone.

"It determines the rest of the week." They enjoyed a bonding moment, then Moira asked, "You okay? You look like I feel."

He got up and moved toward the coffee station in the corner. "Couldn't sleep. You?"

"Same," she answered, throwing her purse on her chair and getting out of her coat.

"I'm almost afraid to ask why." Jack winced a little as he handed her a cup of coffee.

"Paul's in Portland," she informed him, "if that's what you're getting at."

"So it's official? You guys are a thing?"

She gave him an affirming nod. "Weird, huh?"

"Actually, it's not as weird as I thought it would be," he admitted, topping off his own cup. "At least it wasn't a one-night stand."

"Thanks," she said, then qualified, "I think."

"You know what I mean."

Moira studied her brother through a long sip. "So, if that's not keeping you up at night, what is? The boys?"

He conveniently returned to his desk. "I don't want to talk about it."

"But you will." She reached into her purse and produced a white paper bag. "I brought doughnuts."

"I already ate."

"You never eat this early."

"Emily has me on a low-fat diet ever since Dad's heart attack," he told her cheerlessly. "Apparently breakfast is the most important meal of the day."

Moira made a disqualifying buzzing sound with her mouth. "I saw a McDonald's bag in the trash can yesterday." She walked over to his desk and sitting on the edge, handed him a jelly filled donut, his favorite. "What's really going on with you?"

"You tell me. You seem to have all the answers today."

Sighing resignedly, Moira took the bait. "It's Michelle, isn't it?"

Jack didn't answer, just knitted his brow and took a mouthful of the donut, chewing it with deliberate bites.

"She was your first love, Jack. You guys were together for a long time. Through your seminal years. It's natural to feel something when she suddenly drops back into your life."

"I love my wife."

"Whoa." Moira held up a conciliatory hand. "I never said you didn't."

"Sorry." He took a deep breath, blew it out through his nose and confessed, "I keep dreaming about her."

No wonder he wasn't sleeping. "Those memories aren't going to disappear overnight," Moira tried to reassure him. "It took years to build them. It might take years to bury them."

"I mean I keep *dreaming* about her! When I'm awake! When I'm driving! When I'm working!" He jumped up and ran a desperate hand through his hair. "When I go to bed! With Emily! Does that sound natural to you?"

Actually, it sounded like Lindsay when she and Brian were apart. But Moira kept that to herself. "Jack, you need closure."

"Closure!" he countered, slamming his hand on the desk. "I've got two kids, a mortgage and a stay-at-home wife. What more closure could I possibly need?"

"That's not the same," Moira said gently. "I mean with Michelle. You guys never hashed it out. You never gave her the opportunity to explain herself."

"Why the hell should I? One minute we're on a break, which in my mind certainly precluded marrying someone else. If anything it was to make sure we were ready to marry *each other*. I was looking at rings, Moira. Did you know that?" Beginning to pace, he threw his hands out in the air in front of him. "We were saving for a house."

She indulged him in his self-pity session for a few moments. Then she walked over to him and put her hands firmly on his shoulders. "This isn't just about Michelle and how it ended. There's more to it and you know it."

His eyes, forlorn and full of guilt, met hers. She'd always felt closer to Jack than to her older brothers. It went beyond the twin connection; it was as if she knew him better than he knew himself. Or better than he was willing to know himself. They were both thinking it so she said, "You're wondering if Emily hadn't gotten pregnant…"

His jaw tightened and his neck was turning red. "Don't go there, Moira."

"Someone has to. This isn't going to go away on its own, Jack. You need to figure out a way to make it go way. For good. Stop compartmentalizing it and face it."

Jack narrowed his eyes. "Seeing Michelle is the last thing I need."

"It's exactly what you need and sooner rather than later. You can't avoid her forever; Reno isn't that big of a place. You need to make it clear to her that you've moved on. For both of your sakes."

He turned to walk away from her. "No way in hell," he objected angrily.

It was the only way but Moira had to make him come to that conclusion on his own. To get him out of his comfort zone, to make him think it was his idea, to force him to face the fear that part of him still had feelings for his old girlfriend. So she switched gears and asked, "How did you know Emily was different?"

That stopped him in his tracks, shifted his attention back to her. A sappy smile moved across his face. "From the moment I met her, all I wanted was to be with her. I missed her all the time. My thoughts always went back to her. Day and night."

Jackpot. "Do you still feel that way?" Moira prompted.

He shrugged. "Sometimes."

"Did you feel that way about Michelle?"

"It was so long ago, I hardly remember," he told himself as much as Moira. "It was more gradual, I guess. We were..." He searched the room for the word.

"Familiar," Moira finished for him, as a shiver of relevance trickled down her spine.

"I was going to say kids." He collected his thoughts and continued, "Kids becoming adults together, going through the motions, doing what was expected of us."

"Familiar," she repeated as if he hadn't heard.

"No," Jack disagreed with a shake of the head. "Being familiar can be a good thing. The connection, it was different. Or maybe I was different." He seemed to realize that for the first time. "And Emily was so easy to love." He grinned at the memory, wide enough to accentuate the parenthesis around his mouth and the smile lines around his eyes. "I felt like l fell in love with her over and over again."

"That's the difference," Moira pointed out. "Between truly loving someone and being infatuated with them, or just being in love with them. That deeper, stronger, more tangible connection."

"That bullshit might have worked for Paul on you, but it's not that simple for me," he fired back, needlessly going to refill his coffee cup.

"This isn't about me," Moira disputed flatly.

"You sure? Because it sounds awfully...familiar."

Moira willed herself to tread lightly. Her brother was hurting. "You're out of line, Jack."

"And you're projecting."

That threw her little, but she stayed on course. She was making progress. This was the stubborn, recalcitrant, infuriating Jack she knew so well. The Jack that solved problems, not wallowed in them. Time for the kicker. "What do you want me to say? That you were the victim of a nasty case of wanderlust?"

"No!" he shouted. "I want you to say I was the beneficiary of a nasty case of wanderlust!"

"I don't have to," she replied knowingly.

"What?" he baffled.

"You just did." That seemed to strike a chord with him, give him pause. She let out a slow breath and went to him. "Bring home flowers tonight, order take-out, put the boys to bed. Then tell Emily how much you love her. Tell her how glad you are that you married her; how lucky you feel that she's your children's mother. And that it doesn't matter in what order those things happened. Tell her you'd do it all over again. Because I bet you're not the only one who's feeling a little insecure about Michelle being back in town. Maybe part of what's keeping you up at night is all the things left unsaid between you and Emily. Maybe that's where the guilt is really coming from—how she must feel. And maybe she's too afraid to bring it up, too. Too afraid of the answer to pose the question. Reassure her and remind yourself how happy you are in the process."

Jack stared at her in soundless wonder for a full ten seconds. Then he nodded solemnly and she saw the inklings of a smile tug at the corners of his mouth. That signature rule-breaker's grin, carrying with it all of the boyish charm that had wreaked havoc on the resolve of every woman from their mother to his elementary school teachers to Michelle and Emily. To which Moira was thankfully immune. "In other words, don't fuck it all up," she finished pointedly.

He put his arms around her in a brotherly hug. She felt her eyes start to sting as she hugged him back. "Thanks for that. I needed it. And I'm sorry about that crack about Paul. I really am happy for you two. It's just that—"

"I'm your sister and he's your best friend. And if it doesn't work out…"

"Yeah. So don't fuck it all up."

CHAPTER FOURTEEN

Jack's meltdown thwarted, Moira finally turned her attention to work. The rush of the middle of the month was behind her, but Jack had bid on two big jobs already this week. Both were residential quotes, with one property being at the base of Mount Rose. The second job was a teardown in Incline Village, which required prudent hand-holding with the Tahoe Regional Planning Agency. Feeling optimistic about the latter job in particular, she went to the TRPA website and began the application process.

Dealing with Incline Village reminded her of Lindsay and Moira's mind wandered back to their most recent conversation. She'd decided to ignore Jason's friend request on Facebook for now and hadn't heard from him again. Maybe that problem would take care of itself, she told herself half-heartedly. Maybe in the light of day, or days by now, Jason had decided against keeping in touch and seeing her again. He might not want to deal with the potential complications, despite the evening ending well. After all, he'd had two business days to call her at work or even stop by if he was in the area.

Almost an hour later she submitted the TRPA application and moved on to checking email for, unbelievably, the first time today. If Jack needed some information while out in the field he usually communicated with her that way, as did most of their vendors, especially when dealing with credit and billing matters. So it should have come as no surprise to find an email from Jason Parker. Yet for some reason, Moira's stomach dropped and her breath caught in her throat. The subject line said, "Follow-up." She immediately opened it.

Moira,

I hope you had a nice rest of the weekend and didn't work too hard getting the books balanced. It occurred to me on Saturday that we never exchanged cell phone numbers. I sent you a friend request on Facebook, thinking that might be a good way to communicate without being too intrusive. But I know how easily those notifications can slip through the cracks. I'm out-of-town for a couple of days, working my way east, making calls along I-80. I'll be back on Thursday night. I'd love to see you again this weekend. I'm planning to take advantage of the Pineapple Express from last weekend. Are you game? I'm thinking Mt. Rose or Diamond Peak on Saturday.

My contact information is in the signature line at the bottom of the email. Let me know if that works for you.

Jason

Moira stared blankly at the screen. The email had been sent at 6:30 this morning, likely before he started his day on the road. She couldn't deny feeling flattered by the interest. After all, he'd left on Friday night with nothing more than a good night kiss and permission to call her sometime. He'd given her a few days to accept his friend request and when she hadn't, he'd found another discreet way to communicate. She was mentally formulating a response when she noticed another email in the stream. She scrolled up.

To clarify, I meant for the day. :)

Why was she getting so worked up about this? Lindsay was right; all she had to do was say she was seeing someone. It shouldn't come as much of a shock to Jason after the Valentine's Day debacle that there was something between Paul and herself, despite her claim to the contrary. And at the time, she'd been sincere in that assertion. But it did beg the question if Paul hadn't shown up at her door later that night, would she have taken Jason up on his offer of a second date? No, she told herself. She would have found something wrong with him as she had the handful of men who had breezed in and out of her life in the last few years. Fate puts us where we're supposed to be, she reminded herself. And skiing with Jason Parker was definitely not where she was supposed to be.

She wouldn't respond right away; it was only Wednesday and she wanted some time to think about what she should say. She wanted to convey that she was flattered by the invitation, but had to decline. She was seeing someone and regretted not being entirely forthcoming about the status of the relationship. Or, at that time, lack thereof. She flagged the email for easy access later and dove into her inbox. She didn't realize how much time had passed until she was interrupted by the door chimes and a familiar voice.

"Good afternoon, Ms. Brody."

"Hey, Rodney." With a few final pecks on the keyboard, she stood up from behind her desk and approached him with a smile. "Ahead of schedule today?"

"Nope. It's just after four o'clock. Normal time." The balding man let the wind blow the door shut behind him. The stack of boxes in his hands hid his bullet-shaped torso but not his hollow cheeks and sparking blue eyes.

Moira glanced at the clock. "Wow. Time flies when you're having fun," she quipped. "Whatcha got for us today?"

"Looks like office supplies." He set the boxes down on the reception counter. "And something requiring special handling from Portland."

"Jack must have ordered it."

Rodney consulted the tablet in his calloused hand, than scanned the top of the box with it. "It's addressed to you." He offered Moira the stylus and she scribbled her signature across the screen. "And perishable."

"That's odd."

After Rodney left, Moira grabbed scissors and sliced open the top seam of the box. Inside, among the paper wrappings and styrofoam peanuts, she discovered a tower of bakery boxes bound together with ribbon. The tiered boxes each held a different kind of gourmet chocolate. Attached to the top of the smallest box was an envelope addressed to her. She opened it to find a card that read, *Even the sweetest treat isn't as sweet as you, Your Secret Admirer.*

Bringing a hand to her heart, she let herself bask in being wooed for a moment. Paul knew her long-held affinity for sweets, especially dark chocolate. But it admittedly far from rivaled her newfound affinity for him. She found herself fantasizing about him all the time. His mouth, his tongue, his body on hers. She loved being in his arms, loved having his weight on her, loved having him inside her. She'd never considered herself to be salacious, but she couldn't wait for him to come home and take her to bed. And this gesture only added to the want; he'd been thinking about her too. The mere thought made her heart race and her stomach jump. She could get used to this feeling of being loved, wanted, needed. She wouldn't say anything about the gift now, but would thank him properly on Friday night. She opened the top box and indulged in a caramel-filled piece. "Mmm." Or maybe improperly.

She returned to her desk and attempted to reacquaint herself with the matters at hand, but simply couldn't concentrate. Paul was taking up too much real estate in her mind. Finally after thirty unproductive minutes, she decided to call it an early day. She bundled up against the cold and locked up, texting Jack that she was setting the alarm in case he stopped back by. He replied that he was going home early himself, and she hoped he was going to take her advice.

Traffic was light since it was barely five o'clock as Moira headed home. Stopped at a light, she contemplated the fading winter sky and her thoughts once again reverted to Paul. She'd never felt so consumed by someone or something before. Like sex. She loved it. And him. She loved Paul Webster. To absolute distraction. She wanted to feel this way forever, which was amazing, exciting and terrifying all at once. She wondered if he was feeling even half of what she was. If she let herself believe he wasn't, her heart would surely break.

The impatient beep from the car behind her broke her girlish reverie and her tires screeched on the slick pavement as she hurriedly took the turn. Fifteen minutes later she was setting the pastry boxes down on the kitchen counter. She was accustomed to coming home to a dark, empty house on winter nights. But not to the hollow feeling suddenly usurping her stomach. Something was wrong, out of sorts, missing. And that something was, unbelievably, Paul. She'd loved him for so long, but something about him loving her changed everything. She hadn't heard from him all day and imagined he was at a business dinner this evening. She leafed through the mail and poured herself a glass of wine. All she'd had to eat today was a donut with Jack, but her stomach was too jittery to even think about dinner. Normally she would look forward to a cozy evening with Netflix and wine but she couldn't fathom the idea of sitting still. So she decided to brave the cold and go for a walk.

Moira loved her postwar neighborhood with its mature trees and charming bungalows. The streets were quiet tonight, lit only by the rising crescent moon and the amber lights glowing from behind windows. In the four years Moira had lived there the neighborhood had gone through a regeneration of sorts. Young couples and families had replaced some of the older residents, bringing new blood to the area. There was constant remodeling going on and Brody and Sons had done several projects on her street alone.

The walk relaxed her a bit and she brought her wine into the bathroom and warmed up with a long bath, then changed into sweats and got into bed. She'd already traded her pillow for the one Paul had used and she inhaled the lingering scent of him before stacking hers behind it to prop herself up. She flipped on the TV and settled on a rerun of *Seal Team*. The next thing she knew, her eyes began to get heavy and she drifted off to sleep.

The first time she heard a muffled sound from somewhere in the distance, she was caught between the two worlds of sleep and wakefulness. But when she heard it again she was immediately thrust into consciousness. She knew all the noises in this old house. And that wasn't one of them.

Jack had urged her to put in a security system when she first moved in, but she'd never considered it a priority. She'd never once been afraid here. Until now, she thought as panic began to rise inside her. It had been a repetitive grinding sound. Like the garage door opening, she realized, swallowing the lump of terror in her throat. Followed by the sound of a door creaking open, then catching closed again. Then more grinding and a thud. Like the garage door closing.

Had she double-checked the dead bolt on the laundry room door?

Fear-induced adrenaline flooding her body, she bolted to her feet and reached for the Louisville Slugger she kept under the bed with shaking hands. Her eyes darted back and forth in the dim light, then shifted to the nightstand where her phone charged at night. Where the hell was it? Buried somewhere in the bed, she remembered with a sinking heart. She'd fallen asleep with it next to her, waiting for Paul to call. She made the split-second decision not to go for it. Instead, she hid behind the bedroom door and choking up on the bat, laid in wait.

Tears welled in her eyes as she tried to remember the self-defense class her mother had forced her to take before she went away to college. Run, get out, get away was all that came to mind. She could hit the intruder on the head and run to a neighbor's house for help. Unless there were two of them, she realized with fresh horror.

She heard slow, cautious footfalls on the floorboards. Bat held firmly over her shoulder and pulse pounding in her ears, Moira prepared to ambush the intruder from behind. She could see the hallway through the narrow crack of the jamb of the door and she adjusted her eyes to acclimate to the stingy beam of light provided by the streetlight. She was starting to sweat despite the cold night air and her heart was beating outside her chest as she watched a figure emerge from the shadows, advancing toward her and entering the patch of light.

She knew it well.

Heaving a massive sigh of relief, she slumped back against the wall and slid down to the floor. Her heart was still galloping in her chest, but the adrenaline was draining from her body, turning her limbs to rubber. The bat fell from her hands, clattering like a mishandled bowling ball on the hardwood. "Jesus," she managed in a primal whisper, groping for the light switch on the wall above her, illuminating the room along with her unexpected guest. "You scared the shit out of me!"

"I'm sorry." Paul knelt beside her. "I wanted to surprise you."

"What the hell are you doing here?" Moira demanded through shallow breaths.

"I missed you." He scooped her up and stood. "I couldn't wait any longer to see you."

She should be furious, absolutely furious, at him for scaring her like that. But the way he was looking at her melted her heart. She had never seen that look in his eyes before, a mixture of joy and longing to go along with his concerned, yet mischievous grin. It went to her head like champagne, making quick work of her irritation in the process. She simply couldn't stay mad at him. "I thought you weren't coming back until Friday night!"

"I cancelled the rest of my meetings and rented a car," he informed her around a kiss.

"You drove?" she astounded. "From Portland?"

"Uh-huh. Made great time too. A little over eight hours."

"You drove five hundred miles in the snow because you missed me?"

Paul gave her a look of amused annoyance. "Yeah. I kind of hoped you missed me too."

She stroked his cheek, suddenly realizing how much she had. "Of course I missed you. I love you."

"I love you, too. And I want to make love to you. Desperately."

So much so he'd driven through the night, Moira inwardly awed. She put her arms around his neck. "If only I'd worn something other than these old sweats to bed. "

"It's not going to matter in a minute anyway. As sexy as you look in them, they have to go," he said, walking them backward toward the bed.

"What if I'm still mad at you for scaring me?"

"I'll make it up to you."

"You will, huh?" she challenged impishly.

His eyes fired with lust as he eased her down on the bed. "Yeah. In spades." He got out of his travel-wrinkled clothes as she took off her sweats, leaving on her panties.

"Oh, no," he said, laying on top of her. "Those have to go too. I said I was sorry I scared you."

"I know. But you're going to have to work for my forgiveness a little." She reached for him. "I'll let you know when you're paid up." She started stroking him and he responded instantly, quickening and hardening in her hand as that feeling started to build within her, that need to be joined with him.

"Moira," he moaned into her neck. "Don't make me beg. This is all I've been thinking about for the last eight hours."

It wouldn't be long for her either, but she loved knowing she had this power over him, that he wanted her so terribly. He was kissing her throat now, as if trying to pace himself by staying away from the rest of her. And he was losing. "Please."

His hands went to her hips, at the ready to slide her panties down on a moment's notice. "I can't wait another second to bury myself inside you." His tone was gravelly, insistent, breathy.

She granted him permission by covering his hands with hers, then slowly gliding the panties down before spreading her thighs. He entered her with a contented guttural sound, as if it'd been years, not days, since he'd had her. "Oh, yeah. God, yeah," he muttered and began to tunnel inside her. He was throbbing now, filling her with the full length of him, and she raised her buttocks and brought him deeper still. He squatted above her and lifting her legs, rested the backs of her knees in the bend of his elbows. He began to thrust, so hard and fast she could barely catch her breath. Drilling her, increasing the friction between them, flooding her body with electrifying sensations as the tip of him found the most remote part of her. Suddenly she felt spasms engulf her stomach and that arc of gratification begin to build. Digging her fingernails into his back, she let the climax rip through her, take her under, claim her. Just as Paul threw his head back and drained himself into her.

CHAPTER FIFTEEN

Paul awoke to the smell of freshly brewed coffee. The price for which, he supposed, was waking up alone. He sat up, scrubbed his face and stretched his neck. The drive from Portland had been a bitch; he'd had his hands glued to the steering wheel for the last two hours with the low visibility and slippery roads. But, glancing down at the rumpled bed and twisted sheets, it had been worth it. Hands down.

The decision to come home had been a split-second one. And once the idea had gotten into his head, there'd been no getting it out. Moira never left his mind for long these days; she was like a backdrop for all his thoughts. All paths seemed to lead him back to her; her presence in his life was suddenly essential to his functioning.

What the hell was he going to do?

He got out of bed with too long a sigh for a healthy, not quite thirty-year-old and threw on his pants. He headed for the kitchen where he found Moira at the sink. He came up behind her, put his arms around her waist and nuzzled her neck. "Good morning."

She leaned back into the crook of his shoulder. "Good morning."

He indulged in her hair for a few seconds, in her scent, in her warmth. Then he brushed his lips against hers. She tasted like mint and coffee tinged with chocolate. "Not fair. You already brushed your teeth."

"I always brush my teeth first thing. Likely the result of sharing a bathroom with three brothers. I had to make the most of the time I was in there."

Paul left her on a chuckle and poured himself a cup of coffee, then returned to her and freshened hers up. "I tasted chocolate too."

"I usually have a Dove square with my coffee," she explained, putting the wine glass she'd been drying in the cabinet. "But today I had one of your fancy ones. Delish. I never thanked you last night." With a wolfish gleam in her eyes, she laid a kiss squarely on his mouth. "I was distracted. So thank you."

Paul gave her a confused look. "For what?"

"The chocolates. They arrived yesterday."

"I didn't send you chocolates."

"Of course you did." She gestured to the island where several pastel-colored boxes sat. Moving past him, she picked up a small card and handed it to him.

Even the sweetest treat isn't as sweet as you, Your Secret Admirer. Paul read, then met her eyes again. "I didn't send these."

Her expectant gaze became a puzzled frown. "You didn't?"

Paul shook his head. "No."

"Who else would have?"

"I don't know." But he had an idea. And he didn't like it.

She looked down at the card as if the flowery writing held the answer. Then she held one of the boxes up in the air. "But they came from Portland."

Paul felt the hair on the back of his neck stand up as he took the box from her hand. "Portland?" he disconcerted.

"The Sweet Rose Bakery," Moira elaborated.

He'd heard of it; it was an institution in Portland and there were several locations in addition to the original bakery downtown near Pickett's office. But that was immaterial. "Moira, I didn't send you chocolates," he tried again.

She furrowed her brow and stared at him in bewilderment. "Then who did?" She looked around unseeingly for a few seconds, then grabbed her phone off the counter and started typing. "Lindsay, maybe."

"Lindsay?" Paul repeated, fazed. "Why?"

"She does stuff like that sometimes. Maybe the message got lost in translation."

Before Paul could get his head around the possibility, Moira's phone chimed. "No," she relayed, reading the screen. "She has no idea what I'm taking about."

"I have an idea," Paul interjected pointedly. "And he sells windows."

She gave him an exasperated look. "From a bakery in *Portland?"*

Paul didn't give that logic its due credit, just tossed the box down on the counter. "They likely ship everywhere. Pull up the website."

She complied, then handed him the phone. He gave the page a once-over, then hit the highlighted link at the top and held the phone between their heads.

"The Sweet Rose Bakery," answered a singsong voice. "How may I help you?"

"Good morning," Paul said in a businesslike tone. "We received a shipment from your bakery yesterday with no card enclosed. Naturally, we're curious as to the sender."

"I'm sorry about that, sir. That's unusual. Who was the recipient?"

"Brody and Sons Construction. In Reno, Nevada," Paul replied. If he'd said Moira's name they might not be as forthcoming with the information. And he wanted to know just how personal this was. There was a momentary lull, during which Paul could hear chin music from the bakery in the background and the sound of clicking on a keyboard. Finally the woman returned to the conversation. "Hmm. That's odd. I don't show a record of such a shipment going out. Is there another name the order might have been under?"

Paul cleared his throat. This was definitely not business-related. "Moira Brody, perhaps?"

There was more tapping before she came back in a suspicious tone, "Is Ms. Brody available?"

"She's right here," Paul said wryly, giving Moira the phone.

She accepted it, shooting him a look that bordered on pathetic. "Hello? Yes, this is she."

Paul looked on as Moira listened, then shook her head in understanding. "I see. Okay. Thank you. Goodbye."

"Well?"

"They can't give out that information due to privacy laws. The customer wants to remain anonymous."

"She couldn't have told me that?"

"Apparently not." Moira put the phone down and reached out to him, gripping him by the wrists. "We'll figure it out eventually. Let's not worry about it anymore right now."

"Aren't you the least bit curious who your secret admirer is?" he asked sardonically, pulling out of her grasp. "Because I sure as hell am!"

"Paul, this is ridiculous. Are you jealous?"

Was he? It was an unsettling, overpowering, extremely bothersome feeling that he couldn't quite define. "No." His voice faltered a bit. "Should I be?"

"Of course not. But it is kind of cute," she said as the inkling of a smile pulled at the corners of her mouth. "Besides why would Jason, or Window Man as you refer to him, play games like this? He was upfront enough to ask me to dinner and—-" she stopped short.

"And what?"

"It definitely wasn't Jason," Moira said with a revelatory shake of the head. "The email."

"What email?"

Moira began again with an operose sigh, "He sent me an email, asked me to go skiing on Saturday. I—"

"He asked you out again?" Paul interrupted, standing up a little straighter. "When?"

"Yesterday."

There was that bothersome feeling again. "Why didn't you tell me?"

"For one thing, I didn't talk to you yesterday. And it wasn't top of mind when you showed up in the middle of the night." She shrugged nonchalantly. "Does it matter?"

"Hell yes it matters! What did you say?"

"Nothing yet. I wanted to think about how to phrase it. "

"You couldn't have just declined? Said you weren't interested?"

"No!"

"Why not?" Paul raised his voice a notch to match hers.

"Because that's lame, cowardly!"

He shot her a dubious look. "Really, Moira? That's the best you can do?"

She huffed out a breath and went on, a little calmer now, "He calls on us. It's not like I'm never going to see him again. I don't want things to be awkward. I owe him an explanation."

"More like he owes me," Paul aimed a finger at his chest, "an explanation."

"No, Paul, he doesn't," she said firmly.

She was right and he knew it. "You didn't tell him about us?"

"The last time I talked to him there was no us!"

"And when was *that*?"

"Valentine's Day!"

Paul raked a frustrated hand through his hair and tried to get a grip. They were going in circles. He inwardly counted to ten to collect himself then said, "I guess I didn't realize you'd left it so open-ended with him."

"I didn't mean to," she hastened to inform him. Her eyes, only seconds ago full of fire, softened and began to shine. "My life has taken a three-sixty in the last few days. I'm still catching up."

She had no idea. He gathered her into his arms. "Me too."

He held her against him as their breathing leveled off and their heartbeats stabilized. Then Moira stepped out of his embrace, saying, "In the interest of full disclosure, he also sent me a friend request on Facebook. When I didn't accept it, he followed up with the email."

"You must have forgotten to mention that as well," Paul said, the hardness creeping back into his tone.

"No, I intentionally didn't mention it. I didn't want you to think I was trying to make you jealous."

"Why would I be jealous?" he returned derisively. "If there isn't anything to be jealous about?"

"Paul—"

"I'm not doing this again," he heard himself say and instantly regretted it.

He watched Moira's expression fall and hurt fill her eyes. "Is that was this is really about? Lindsay?"

"No." He grabbed her arm just as she was turning away. "This is about us. You and me. Is it ever going to be just you and me? Without Lindsay or anyone else lurking in the background?"

Moira's face became a confused frown. "What are you talking about?"

"I bet you told Lindsay about the friend request, the chocolates, the ski date right away."

She sniffed the air, then answered in a superior tone, "As a matter of fact, I haven't had the chance. I've been a little *distracted* since I got the chocolates and the email yesterday afternoon. But yes, I told her about the friend request. Jason and I never exchanged cell numbers. Over the weekend, it was the only way he had to contact me."

Paul had to admit that was reasonable. "And her advice was to keep it to yourself?"

"Actually, she suggested I accept it as a vehicle for telling him that I was seeing someone. Not everything is about you, Paul. I'm sure it never occurred to Lindsay that something as innocuous as a friend request would be a problem. You and Lindsay are friends on Facebook, aren't you?"

What did that have to do with anything? "Yes, of course."

"You had a much more serious romantic relationship with her than I ever had with Jason. As she pointed out, all I did was kiss him good night." Moira crossed her arms over her chest and gave him a recriminating look. "Not ask him to marry me."

"That's irrelevant," Paul fired back in equal measure.

"It's entirely relevant. You want it to just be about you and me? That'll have to start with you." She grabbed her phone off the counter. "I have to get ready for work." She turned on her heel and stormed out of the kitchen.

Paul stood as if frozen, watching her go. He was being an ass and they both knew it. He considered himself to be pretty stable, confident, levelheaded. Even after all the bullshit with Lindsay. But he had never felt so insecure, so vulnerable, so out of control of his emotions as he had lately. He took a sip of coffee, wishing it were a shot of whiskey, swore under his breath and headed down the hall.

He found Moira in the bedroom, staring blankly into her jam-packed closet.

He came up behind her, repeatedly reminding himself not to touch her. "I'm sorry. I don't know how to do this, to be with you like this, to love you this way."

She didn't say anything, just let out a deep breath and kept looking straight ahead. He was about to speak again when she turned slowly around. The hurt was planted deeply in her eyes now and she replied in a watery voice, "Neither do I. Can't we try to figure it out together?"

"We have to. I can hardly be away from you for a few hours, let alone a few days." She smiled at him then, big enough to narrow her eyes and flash her dimples. He leaned down to kiss her and felt that tug in his stomach, that pull on his heartstrings as his world righted itself. This kiss was different; lazy instead of rushed, more sensual than sexual, tender, not urgent. They wouldn't end up in bed after this, but go on with their day, knowing they'd see each other tonight. They broke apart and Paul rested his forehead against hers with a sigh. "Skiing, huh?"

"Paul..." she said, tilting her head back around a giggle.

"I ski, you know," he maintained. "It's just not my favorite thing, so I don't make the time."

Moira put her arms around his neck and gave him a playful grin. "What is your favorite thing?"

He stunned himself by saying, "Being here, like this, with you."

His words seemed to surprise her as much as they had him. She swallowed hard and said, "I'll take that over skiing any day."

*****

"You okay?" Jack asked Moira later that morning.

"I'm fine. I texted you," she replied, heading for the coffee maker. "You said you'd be in this morning."

"I know. It's just unlike you to be late." He looked up at her with a boyish grin. "I brought donuts."

"Someone's in a good mood," Moira remarked, grabbing a powdered sugar donut from the box. "Take my advice?"

"That I did," he said a little too cheerfully. "Slept like a baby, too."

"You're welcome by the way."

He got up and met Moira halfway as she was heading to her desk. He bent down and kissed her on the cheek. "Thanks."

Smiling, she watched him walk to the copier on the far side of the office. He drove her crazy half the time, but he was such a good guy, so solid like their father. Emily was just as lucky as he was. Of course she'd never tell him that.

"I wanted to talk to you about something." He turned around to face her as the copier whirred behind him. "With Dad stepping back a bit and busy season just around the corner, maybe we should consider hiring someone part-time. I have a good feeling about those two bids, especially the teardown in Incline. I can't be in two places at once and you never get a break during the day. Kevin and Pat don't have any interest in working in the business; Dad was a little optimistic when he named the place. Mornings like today, when you're running late or have an appointment, are bound to happen from time to time. If I'm out and about no one is here to mind the store, cover the phones."

He had a good point. Nodding, Moira said, "I agree. Mom helped out some over the years, and then all of us in high school and college. We were managing okay with three of us, but if it's mostly going to be you and me going forward, we'll need some help."

Jack grabbed the copies off the machine and when he turned back to her, his expression had sobered a bit. "I think we have to face the fact that Dad will never be back in a full-time capacity. He's already had a close call and it would be nice for he and Mom to do some traveling, exploring, before they get too old. He would never suggest this, but I bet he would agree if we presented the idea. It might even come as a relief to him, lengthen his life."

"Do people still look for jobs in the classifieds? I can place an ad, post something on our website."

"Okay. Thanks." He threw the copies in his backpack and zipped it up. "I know you just applied for the TRPA permit, but I'm going to run up to Incline, double-check my calculations. This could be a huge feather in our cap. A multi-year project. And," he met her gaze enthusiastically, "they haven't hired an architect yet. The drawings submitted by a friend's firm didn't meet their expectations. I gave them Paul's number. I'm going to call him on my way up there and suggest he follow-up with them when he gets back."

Moira cleared her throat. "He got back last night."

Jack's mouth broke into a sneaky smile. "That bastard. No wonder you were late this morning."

"Actually, that's not why. But it did have something to do with Paul." She brought him up to speed on the chocolates and Paul's reaction.

Her brother's face clouded and his jaw tightened. "Who could it be?"

"I have no idea. But Paul thinks he does. How much do you know about Jason Parker?" Moira asked, holding his concerned gaze.

"From Sun?" Jack shrugged. "He's called on us for a couple of years. He's kind of a ski bum who works to live, unlike most of us who live to work. Why?"

Moira summed up the events of Friday night.

After a moment of consideration, he put in, "He did ask me about you."

She stared at him in openmouthed wonder, then exclaimed, "Why didn't you tell me?"

"Tell you what?"

He was impossible. "That he asked about me!"

"What's there to tell? He asked me if you were in a relationship. I said no. Ball's back in his court," he finished dismissively.

"When was *that?*" she exasperated.

Jack mulled that over then replied, "Over the summer, I think."

Moira wanted to kill him. "Before or after Lindsay's wedding?"

He reached into the back pocket of his jeans and produced his phone, searched on it, then informed her, "It was the beginning of August. He took me to lunch and your name came up."

"So, it was after the wedding."

"What does that have to do with anything?"

Moira wasn't sure but she knew she was beside herself. "I can't believe you didn't tell me!"

Jack let out a tired sigh. "I mentioned it to Emily and she told me to leave it alone. She said it looked like you and Paul were finally getting somewhere and if I screwed it up she would never forgive me. Not to mention Lindsay."He shook his head defeatedly. "I don't know how you women know these things. All this intuitive bullshit is lost on me."

Now Moira was even more perplexed. Jason doing this simply didn't add up in her mind. It had taken him months after asking Jack about her to invite her to dinner, and on Valentine's Day no less. Despite the drama of the evening, he'd followed-up the next day. Then waited a few days before contacting her again. Why would he send her chocolates anonymously? He'd want her to know they were from him, want her to know he'd been thinking about her. "Jack, I don't think he would do this. He was forward enough to ask me out, stay in touch. Why play games like this?"

"The thrill of the chase." Jack's eyes fired mischievously. "As long as somebody's keeping score, it's on."

She folded her arms across her chest. "So he's only interested in me because someone else is?"

Jack shrugged into his coat. "No, he's interested in you because you're beautiful and smart. Which you happen to come by honestly," he continued, grabbing his keys off the desk. "The temper like a switch not so much."

And we're back. But Moira knew it was his way. "Which I also happen to come by honestly. So what do I do now? He asked me to go skiing on Saturday."

"Since you're seeing Paul, I assume you won't be going. Just tell him that. If he sent the chocolates, that should put an end to it. He seems like a reasonable guy, not a stalker or anything."

He paused at the door for a moment. "Although I will say, it's quite a coincidence they came from Portland."

"Yeah," Moira muttered under her breath, watching Jack leave. Then she sat down at her desk and opened her email. Might as well get it over with. Short and sweet.

Jason,

Thank you for reaching out. I hope your week has been productive. I appreciate the offer of skiing on Saturday, but I'll have to decline. I should have been more forthcoming on Friday night. Paul and I have a lot of history between us and yet never really defined our relationship. That changed this weekend rather suddenly.

You should know that this has no bearing whatsoever on your professional relationship with Brody and Sons.

Thanks again for the invite. Enjoy the fresh powder!

Moira

She stared at the computer monitor for a long moment, then hit send. She watched the screen reset and leaned back in her chair with a sigh. She should feel a sense of relief that was behind her. But for some reason, she had a portentous feeling it wasn't over quite yet.

*****

Jack took the turn onto Mount Rose Highway and started up the mountain to Incline Village. He had chains in the truck, but he wouldn't need them. The lanes had been cleared, the result of which was piled high on each side of the road, creating a wall of snow and ice. He estimated it to be about ten feet, average during a typical winter. He'd seen twice that, half that and almost nothing at all in his lifetime. The years of drought were always scary ones, seeming to siphon the lake and take with it Tahoe's plethora of winter activities for tourists and locals alike. And in the worst of years, even those of the ensuing summer. But the last few winters had been good to the basin, providing enough snowmelt to keep the lake at its normal level and temperature. And its hallmark shade of blue.

He couldn't wait until his boys were old enough to get up on skis. Maybe by next winter they could try a little cross-country, work their way up to bunny hills and lessons. He'd grown up skiing and sledding in Tahoe in the winter and enjoying the beach and lake in the summer. He and Emily had brought the boys up to sled at Christmastime, but things had been so crazy since his father's heart attack at the first of the year, he hadn't had the time since.

He let out a restorative breath. He'd actually gotten a decent night's sleep, despite he and Emily making love until midnight. Thank God he had Moira to talk him off the ledge, bring him back to reality and what really mattered. He couldn't ask for a better wife and mother than he and the boys had in Emily. It had all happened so fast with her. They'd hit it off right away, meeting through her cousin whom he had known at UNLV. Despite both being generationally from Reno, they didn't know each other or have any friends in common. She was two years younger and had gone to Catholic schools and he to public. She had attended Sierra Nevada College, wanting to stay close to home. She was close to her family, her mother in particular, and had no desire to go to school far away, let alone live anywhere else afterward.

Jack, on the other hand, had other plans. He'd received a scholarship for college and once he'd gotten the partying out of his system freshman year, had maintained a 4.0. He'd earned a business degree and was job hunting in major cities all over the West. But the economy had crashed during his college years, affecting the family business as well as the job market he'd graduated into. Coming back home to help out Brody and Sons was supposed to be a temporary solution for both his dad and himself.

And of course there was Michelle.

They'd known each other since middle school, hanging in the same group of friends into high school. He'd played football and baseball with her brother and their parents had been friends socially. It was actually at his mother's urging that he asked her to Homecoming junior year. After that, one thing let to another. The next thing he knew they were going out, sometimes alone, sometimes in a group. They lost their virginity to each other the night of Junior Prom in her parent's basement. They went to different colleges, with Michelle going out-of-state. They had agreed to see other people if the situation presented itself but to be forthcoming about it, especially if the relationship was heading in a sexual direction. She'd accepted a few dates, he'd asked a few girls out. But dating other people never went anywhere for either one of them. She transferred to UNLV after sophomore year and despite each having their own apartment, all but lived together for the next two years.

She'd landed back home after graduation, also at loose ends. They fell into a rhythm of seeing each other most evenings, spending the weekends together, both adjusting to living at home again. Sometimes he would get a room just so they could have some privacy, a luxury they'd gotten used to in college. He found himself missing her at night when he went to bed, not just for the obvious reason, but for the emptiness of it. Ultimately he stopped looking for a job elsewhere, becoming more and more invested in his father's business. Michelle got an entry-level position with a pharmaceutical company and started traveling, some weeks being gone a night or two.

Eventually he got an apartment in South Reno, with easy access to the mountain. Michelle would often stay over and they were in constant contact, coordinating schedules, plans, family functions. It was a given, to their families as much as to themselves, that they would get married and settle in Reno in due time. Michelle was career-oriented and her travel would only increase as her territory did, something Jack would have to get used to. She was smart and ambitious and presented well, the perfect combination for pharmaceutical sales.

It was also the perfect combination for trouble.

He still couldn't quite put his finger on the time line, but in retrospect there'd been a shift in their relationship, in her. She was spending more time on the road, raking in huge bonuses and often working at night on her laptop. He'd brought up the idea of moving in together, maybe getting a bigger place, but she'd said between her traveling and his place, there was no need. She couldn't imagine finding the time to move right now, with so much going on at work. Besides, her saving money by living at home would enable them to have a bigger down payment for a house someday.

Things went along like that for a year or so, with Michelle earning a promotion to territory manager and he taking on more responsibility in the business. Moira, who had intended to spread her wings after graduation, had also started working for their father. Paul had opened up his own firm; Lindsay was living in San Francisco. He and Moira were together a lot during the day. She was actually the first one to point out that Michelle wasn't around as much as usual. She asked if something was up and he'd told her she was busy with work.

Then, seemingly out of the blue, Michelle told him she wanted a break like they'd taken freshman year of college. She wanted to be honest with him; she was attracted to a guy at work. He'd asked her out and she'd declined, but she couldn't get him out of her mind. They'd had a drink after a team building activity and he'd walked her back to her room. He'd reiterated his interest in her and had given her a kiss on the cheek. She said she needed to know if it was the flattery of the offer, the attention, or if something was really there. She couldn't take the next step with him until she knew for sure. It wouldn't be fair to either one of them.

Jack had been floored. Despite sensing her restlessness, the slight change in her attitude, they were staying together most nights when she was in town and spending most of their free time together. He'd talked to her sister about rings, had saved enough money for a decent-sized diamond. He'd had no choice but to agree to the break, but personally had no desire to see anyone else. Most of him thought it was just the idea of freedom that was appealing to her and that it would quickly pass.

He'd been wrong.

The months that followed had been prophetic. She was traveling more and more and working on the weekends. Writing reports, planning for the upcoming week, entertaining clients. She was having the time of her life, according to her social media posts.

And he was in hell.

When he'd asked her how she was feeling about things, she'd admitted she was seeing the man from work and had kissed him, but nothing more. He heard the conflict in her voice that echoed the one in his heart. He loved her, he wanted her back. But he wasn't going to share her, especially in bed.

It was right before Christmas of that year when she'd said she still wasn't ready to get back together, let alone make a lifelong commitment. She loved him but something was holding her back. She didn't know if it was the finality of marriage, or if she'd outgrown him and life in Reno. She was confused and needed some space.

Three months later she got married in Vegas.

It had been an impulsive decision, she had told him. She'd called him first, before she'd even told her parents, out of respect. She would always love him in her own way, Jack recalled her saying, taking the next curve a little faster than he should have.

He had been absolutely devastated. Paul and Moira had been there for him, of course. But neither one of them had ever had a relationship nearly as serious as he and Michelle's, so as well-intentioned as they were, it was hard for them to relate. His family was also very supportive, even in their shock. Michelle's parents had been mortified; they'd never even met this guy. He'd had no desire to date, to take friends up on their offers of getting set up or to go the online route. His mother would repeatedly tell him someday it would all make sense, there was a reason for it, he had to keep the faith. He pretended to believe her.

And then he met Emily.

The instant he saw her, before she even said a word to him, the weight on his heart suddenly lifted. She had the brightest smile of anyone he'd ever met, the most beautiful brown eyes he'd ever seen. He simply couldn't take his eyes off of her. They talked in the corner of a bar for hours and he offered to take her home when her friends wanted to leave because he wanted her to stay. She'd been understandably leery about that, but with her cousin's endorsement, she'd agreed. They closed the place down, then talked in his car in front of her house for another hour. He called her the next day and asked her to dinner. A week later, he sent his mother flowers to thank her for not letting him give up.

He told her all about Michelle; Emily was the only other person who knew all the gory details. She'd had a serious boyfriend in college for a couple of years herself, but it had fizzled after graduation.

She hadn't dated anyone seriously since. He told her he loved her within a month of meeting her and she started staying over at his apartment every weekend and occasionally during the week.He was going to ask her to move in with him but before he could, she realized she was pregnant. They'd been together for four months.

She'd been acting a little differently, more distant, all of the sudden. Jack wouldn't let himself believe history was repeating itself and remembering what his mother had said about keeping the faith, he asked her straight-out what was going on. She told him through tears and wringing hands that she was pregnant. She'd known for a week but had been afraid to tell him. She didn't want him to think she was trying to trap him or worse yet, risk losing him. And once he got over the initial shock, he was actually thrilled. He told her, realizing it himself for the first time, that she could never lose him. He loved her unconditionally and amazingly, she loved him with equal measure. They found out they were having twins two months later. He used most of his savings for a down payment on a house and the rest for an engagement ring. And those were the two best decisions he'd ever made, Jack reminded himself, feeling a smile spread to his eyes and intensify. Along with meeting his college buddy at the bar that night, of course.

So why did his world suddenly turn upside down when Michelle moved back to town? He'd go for months without her even crossing his mind, despite reminders of their years together all around him. Moira said it was natural, that the history would always be there and would occasionally rear its ugly head. That he had to see Michelle, get it over with, to prove to himself that there was nothing lingering between them. But what would be the point of that? He couldn't be any happier than he was in his life with Emily and he didn't want to upset her by saying he needed to see his old girlfriend for closure. He'd gone through hell with one woman to earn heaven with another. And he wasn't going to do anything to jeopardize that. But Moira said if he didn't... The ring of his phone broke his retrospection. "I was just about to call you," Jack said by way of greeting, shelving the past for the time being.

"Well, I'm saving you trouble."

Jack had a feeling this was going to be about chocolates. "You have the floor."

"Have you talked to Moira today?"

"I just left her at the office."

"Did she tell you about her special delivery?" Paul asked mockingly.

"I was brought into the secret admirer fold, yes."

"Don't you find it worrisome?"

"Obviously not as worrisome as you do."

"How well do you know this window guy?"

"He's called on us for a couple of years, taken me to lunch a few times. Seems like a nice enough guy. Full disclosure, he asked me about Moira over the summer. I was just scolded for not making that public knowledge sooner."

"Asked about her how?" Paul's tone was suspicious.

"If she was seeing anyone. I said no. Sure took him long enough to do something about it."

Paul was quiet for so long that Jack thought the call might have dropped. Finally, he said, "Yeah, well I inadvertently met him the night he decided *to* do something about it. But that's another story. I'm more concerned about this secret admirer bullshit. Do you think it's him?"

"I don't know. Moira has a good point. Why would he beat around the bush like that? He was upfront enough to ask her out again."

"Either way, I don't like it. It smells fishy to me."

Jack let out a resigned breath. "Want me to call him? See if I can get a read?" If it wasn't his sister they were talking about, he'd probably get a kick out of seeing Paul all tied up in knots.

"Damn right I want you to call him! You want to get to the bottom of this too, don't you?"

"Not as badly as you do apparently."

Paul ignored the jab, saying, "I also wanted to see if you can spare Moira for a few days next week."

"I'm not her keeper. You'll have to take that up with her. You and I both know she runs the place."

"True. But before I ask her, I want to make sure you'll be around, have coverage."

"I can be. Or have the phones forwarded to my cell." Just another example, Jack thought, of why they needed to hire some office help. Moira deserved a life outside of Brody and Sons.

"Great. Thanks."

"Let me guess," Jack said, entering the Incline Village city limits. "You're going skiing."

"So you got the full briefing. I'd actually been thinking about it anyway. Just haven't made the time. And it's ski week. Lots going on up there."

"Aha."

"You said you were going to call me?" Paul changed the subject.

"Yeah. I bid on a big job—a teardown in Incline. They're looking for an architect. I gave them your number. They're going to check out your website, give you a call if it looks like a fit."

"Thanks. I'd love a stab at it."

Jack shoved the truck into park. "I'm up here now. I'm going to have another look around, rerun my numbers. I want to be prepared if they entertain other bids."

"Text me their contact information so I can follow-up."

"I just did," he said, taking his phone off speaker. "Give them a day or two to look at your portfolio

146

before you contact them. But they don't seem to be the beat around the bush type, so they might be in touch before that."

"Speaking of beating around the bush…"

"I'll call him on my way back down. I'll let you know what I find out."

"Thanks."

They disconnected and Jack grabbed his backpack from the passenger seat with a shake of the head. "I almost feel sorry for the guy," he said to no one. "Now he's going to be the one being chased."

CHAPTER SIXTEEN

"Speaking of skiing, I still haven't heard back from Jason Parker," Moira informed Paul. They were heading up to Squaw Valley for a few days. Paul had booked a suite in the Village, something for which he likely paid dearly this time of year. Moira found it notable that they would be on the California side of the lake, a hour from Diamond Peak or Mt. Rose, popular with locals like themselves. When she'd pointed that out, he'd reminded her that Squaw had more slope-side lodging and dining options. While that was true, she had a feeling it had more to do with her first skiing invitation of the weekend. It was also interesting that they were going on Sunday instead of Saturday, despite, as Paul maintained, it being ski week.

"Maybe he's a sore loser," Paul said without taking his eyes off the road. "Can't deal with rejection."

"He's usually more responsive. It's unprofessional," Moira continued, ignoring the snappish remark. "He didn't return Jack's call from last week either." She glanced over at him. "But I bet you already knew that."

Paul met her perceptive gaze with a loaded one. "Yeah, I already knew that," he confirmed, turning his attention back to the road.

Moira could do nothing but shake her head. Men. They seemed to have a code all their own. And in Paul's mind, Jason Parker had broken it. Which of course wasn't the case at all; he had no idea how Paul really felt about her. No more than she did. Well, maybe she'd had some idea, but she certainly didn't think he loved her. She really hadn't been surprised when he brought up going skiing. Paul, like her brothers, was nothing if not competitive. But three days at Squaw seemed a bit excessive. Added to which, he'd been more reserved lately, like he had something weighing heavily on his mind. This morning was no exception, so she decided to ask him about it. "Paul, is everything okay?"

He gave her a puzzled frown. "Yeah. Why?"

"You've seemed different the last few days."

"Different? How?"

It took Moira a moment to put the observation into words. "Preoccupied, a little distant. Ever since you got back from Portland."

His face broke into a facetious grin. "You mean ever since the night I drove eight hours in the remnants of a blizzard because I couldn't wait another forty-eight hours to see you?"

She had to give him that. "Yeah."

"And we've spent every night together since then."

"I know." She hesitated, then asked, "Do you need some space?"

"No. If I did would I have asked you to go away for the weekend?"

"No, I guess not," she replied with a shrug.

They rode in companionable silence for a while and Moira tried to relax and take in the scenery. The frosted pine trees dotting the pristine mid-mountain hills, the crystal blue sky, the jagged, pearly peaks were breathtaking no matter how many times she'd seen them.

"Do you?" Paul was asking.

Moira shook off the reverie. "What?" she replied, turning to face him.

"Need some space?" he wanted to know, staring straight ahead.

"No, of course not. We've only just found each other."

He laid his hand over hers and squeezed it gently. "Yeah, I know. I do have some things on my mind though. Nothing for you to worry about."

"But it has nothing to do with windows, right? Other than maybe prompting this ski trip?"

Paul took his time in replying. "No. I mean, I don't like the idea of him pursuing you on a couple of levels. And while it might have pushed me to go skiing again, I'm not jealous of him. If anything, I'm grateful to him. For forcing me to tell you how I feel, for forcing me to realize it for myself. Because now I know that you feel the same way. And otherwise we wouldn't be here, together, like this. But I don't like the idea of him, or anybody else, sending you chocolates or inviting you to go skiing or taking you to dinner."

Moira shifted her body toward him as much as the seat belt would allow. "Paul, neither do I."

"I know. But for some reason, that doesn't make me like it any more. It's out of character for me and frankly, something I'm not proud of. But so is feeling this way. Not just about you, but about anybody." He turned his head and met her gaze. "Because I've never felt this way before. So I guess I'll just have to get used to it."

Moira felt her heart swell in her chest. "I could get used to it."

"That's good. Because I don't think it's going to change any time soon."

Moira didn't think it was ever going to change for her. And that terrified her as much as it delighted her. She wondered if he felt that way too.

"I'm not possessive or paranoid by nature and I don't intend to become that way now," Paul kept going. "But I think it's creepy that someone is sending you chocolates anonymously. I'd actually be relieved if it was him because according to Jack he's a decent guy who will likely get the message and move on. But if he doesn't or if it isn't him, I find it a little disturbing. And even if our relationship hadn't evolved, I'd be just as concerned as your friend as I am as your boyfriend."

Moira sucked in a breath. That was the first time either one of them had verbally defined their relationship. It was assumed, she supposed, that it was monogamous, serious. But for some reason, hearing it out loud made it official, real. She let that sink in for a moment, let the wonder of it fill her heart and settle, then said, "Well I'm neither one of those things either. And I'm certainly not used to being someone's girlfriend, let alone being possessed by someone. So I guess we'll both just have to get used to it."

Paul didn't respond, only shook his head thoughtfully. And the next thing she knew they were slowing down and he was pulling over on the narrow shoulder of Highway 89, just short of the entrance to the resort. He put the car in park and released his seat belt, then leaned across the center console, lifted her chin with his finger and took her mouth a prolonged, heartfelt kiss. Moira felt the pull in the pit of her stomach, the butterflies start to swarm around it, then her heart begin to soar in her chest. And if she hadn't known before, she knew then. He would be it for her. He would be her husband, her children's father, they would grow old together. Her eyes stung with the realization as he slowly pulled his mouth away. Then he looked deeply into her eyes and said, "I don't seem to have any choice but to get used to it. I'm counting on you coming to that same conclusion."

"I think I just did," she heard herself say, holding his gaze. She tried to swallow the lump in her throat, but it continued to grow and spread, filling her with a joy like she had never known. "Paul," she managed, her voice barely above a whisper, "what's happening to us?"

"I think this is what it feels like to fall in love with someone over and over again," he replied in kind.

"I like it," she told him, remembering what Jack had said about Emily. "Do you think it'll keep happening?"

"Yeah, I think so," he answered with a chuckle in his eyes.

"Good," she said. "Because I'm counting on it."

With a peck on the lips they broke apart and Paul began driving again. They turned off the highway and wound through the residential section of Squaw Valley where chalet-style homes peppered the hills and meadows. Within five minutes they pulled up to the main entrance of the resort. The A-frame building resembled an Alpine ski lodge and appeared to have changed very little since it was built for the Olympics in 1960.

"Do you want to wait here while I check in? Our cabin is toward the back, since it's a ski-in/ski-out. It'll save you from having to get right back into the car again."

"I'll go in. I've never been here. I'd like to check it out."

Paul jolted back in surprise. "You haven't?"

"No. Squaw Valley was a little high-end for the Brodys." Raising her eyebrows, she tossed him an oblique look. "We'd come up to ski for the day or even a half-day sometimes, usually to Mt. Rose. Then Diamond Peak, mostly with you guys, when I got older. My mom never liked skiing much; she prefers Tahoe in the summer like you do. But Dad says the summer is a waste of the mountains. No fun just looking at them."

"He has a point, I guess," Paul said around a laugh, zipping up his jacket. "A lot of people prefer Tahoe in the winter. In fact, the only reason I got this reservation was a last-minute cancellation." So saying, he got out of the car and before Moira could collect her purse, he was at the passenger side opening the door for her. They walked into the lobby hand in hand and headed for the front desk.

The reception area decor mirrored that of the exterior. They were given their room assignment by a cheerful clerk who invited them to enter a contest to choose a new name for the resort. There were plaques and pictures on the walls detailing the history of the Valley as well as that of the Tahoe Basin and the Native Americans who'd called it home for centuries. Moira found it all fascinating, but Paul seemed quiet again as they drove to their cabin. She decided to let it go for now but even if she hadn't, she would have been forgotten to mention it once they got there. Because the instant she saw the place she was blown away.

The term cabin was at best a modest description. The lodge-style motif was beautiful in its own right, but the finishing touches reminded Moira more of a model home than a ski cabin. The gray, repetitive hue wood floors sat in perfect contrast to the white oak cabinets in the stainless steel kitchen and the mid-century furnishings gave it a clean, modern look. But it was the stacked stone fireplace and thick wooden beams on the ceiling that brought it all together, gave it the texture and feel of Tahoe. And the great room and kitchen were only the beginning. There were three bedrooms outfitted in similar fashion, each with its own bathroom as well as a formal dining room, all with mountain views. And a private deck with a hot tub. "Paul, this is incredible," Moira amazed, struggling to take it all in.

"It was all they had. I hope it'll due," he said, coming up behind her and placing his hands on her shoulders.

"It's big enough for a dozen people!"

"Ten, actually. I think the third bedroom has bunk beds."

She leaned back against him. "Thank you."

"Fully stocked kitchen if we don't feel like going out." He turned her around to face him. "Which we may not after a long day on the mountain."

"I'm fine with staying in. The hot tub looks interesting," she said, suddenly feeling naughty.

"Great minds think alike." He laid a solid kiss on her mouth. "Now let's go skiing. We're burning daylight."

*****

"Since when are you so good?" Moira asked Paul later that afternoon. They were skiing down a blue square piste surrounded by black diamond chutes and corduroy runs. And she was falling more than skiing. Paul, on the other hand, was practically Bode Miller.

"Skiing has grown on me," he answered nonchalantly.

"Not this much," she contended.

"I guess I needed some motivation."

"Or some competition," Moira put in wryly.

Helping her up, he drew her to him despite the layers of ski gear between them. "I didn't think I had any."

"You don't and you know it. But either way, you're kicking my ass."

He slid his goggles over his helmet, then did the same with hers. "We can even the score later," he told her with the devil dancing in his eyes. "And I like your ass just the way it is."

"Promises, promises." Moira matched his tone, rich in innuendo. She could feel the wind-driven snowflakes scrape her face, the sting of the near-freezing temperatures nip at her nose, but the furnace inside her was revving up again, stopping the chill dead in its tracks. She linked her arms around his neck, brought him closer. She still had to remind herself this was Paul who was turning her insides into pulp, Paul who was responsible for the push and pull in the pit of her stomach, Paul who seemed to look into her very soul and find a dormant part of her. It was as if everything had suddenly changed between them, but was still wonderfully the same. His lips were hovering overs hers when she heard someone clear their throat behind her.

"Going back up, folks?" asked a tentative voice. "Second to last run of the day."

With a defeated breath Paul pulled back. "No," he answered without turning away from her. "I think we're done for today."

"Don't miss the sunset," the man suggested. "Last night was incredible."

Paul looked directly into Moira's eyes. "It sure was."

"The resort has several decks," he was still talking. "Heat lamps, fire pits, awesome views of the mountains and the valley."

"Thanks," Paul said. "But we have our own accommodations."

They exchanged parting words with the ski patrolman after which Paul asked Moira, "Ready?"

"Yeah. Maybe tomorrow will be a better day."

They finished out the run and skied back to the cabin. They secured their skis and poles just outside and hung the rest of their gear in the mudroom. Paul started a fire in the fireplace on the deck and opened a bottle of wine while Moira surveyed the contents of the refrigerator. He wasn't exaggerating when he said the kitchen was fully stocked. Good thing because she was starving from skiing, or lack thereof, and Paul likely was too.

Moira was still staring at the fridge, debating their options, when Paul came in and handed her a glass of wine. "Well?"

"Do you have any idea how to make your mom's lasagna? You must have chosen the Italian package; there are all kinds of pasta noodles, sauces and cheeses. No ground meat, though. But we could make do."

"I can text her, ask her to send me the recipe or how to improvise."

Something suddenly occurred to Moira. "Did you tell your parents about us?"

Paul stiffened a bit. "Not yet. Did you?"

"Not in so many words. I told my mom I was going skiing for a couple of days. She asked with whom and I told her. She didn't say anything for a few seconds, then asked who else was going. I said just you and me." Moira smiled at the recollection. "She thought it was great, told me it was a long time coming. Honestly, were we the last ones to know?"

"Apparently," he said, hooking her by the waist and bringing her to him. "We have a lot of time to make up for. But I have an idea how we can do that."

"You do, huh?"

"Yeah, I'll show you after dinner." He left her with a kiss and grabbed his phone off the counter. "I'll text my mom. It would be fun to cook together. We've never done that before."

They hadn't done a lot of things together until recently, Moira thought. And she hoped there was much more of that to come. She was gaining confidence in bed and wanted to give him anything and everything he wanted before he could ask for it, like he was doing for her. "I'll get the noodles started. That much I know." They worked in the kitchen companionably for almost an hour, drinking wine and making the lasagna. Paul doctored the jarred sauce while Moira dealt with the pasta and the cheese. Once the noodles were done, they put it all together. Now they were sitting in the hot tub with their second bottle of Cabernet and a charcuterie tray while the lasagna baked.

Naked.

"Too bad we missed the sunset," Moira commented.

"There'll be one tomorrow night."

"It's also too bad you neglected to mention there was a hot tub. I would have brought my swimsuit."

"I've been so forgetful lately," Paul said with a wolfish grin, topping off their glasses and returning to her side.

"Hmm. And forgot to pack one for yourself as well. So unlike you."

"Yeah." He shifted his body to face her. "It really is."

Narrowing her eyes in mocked irritation, Moira nodded skeptically. "And very convenient."

"I prefer opportunistic." Taking the wine glass out of her hand and setting it down on the rim of the hot tub, he went on cleverly, "One of the reasons I liked this unit was the privacy." He tipped his head toward the rock wall surrounding the inner part of the deck, then started nibbling on her neck, just below her earlobe. "And I'm counting on it being every bit as private as advertised. Because I want to do some very private things to you. If it's all the same to you."

"You can do anything you want to me." She told him, tilting her head to one side to give him full access. "In private or anywhere else."

That seemed to strike a chord with him, give him momentary pause. Then his tongue started moving down her throat, slowly licking its way, until it reached the valley between her breasts. He cupped them, slick and wet from the bubbles, and began to fondle her. His thumbs were working her nipples to a point and she felt a quiver of desire start to roll through her. "Paul," she murmured, leaning her head back.

"Tell me what you want. Tell me what to do to you."

"Suck on them," she surprised herself by saying.

He took one in his mouth, still massaging the other, and pulled, bit, sucked. She felt the building ache consume her pelvis, the urge to be filled with him start to spread throughout her body. His hands slid down to her waist and he brought her against him. She could feel his erection against her thigh and she began to stroke him but he quieted her hand with his.

"Let's try something different. Something I've never done before either." He stood and turned her around in the foamy water and braced her hands against the side of the hot tub.His fingers found her and began to explore, crease by crease, pleat by pleat, fold by fold. Her fleshy core began to swell and she wanted to reach for him, but his fingers were inside her now and she began to rock back and forth, grinding against him, bringing them deeper into her. She had never felt so helpless, so aroused, so out of control. Suddenly waves of pleasure overtook her, touched every corner of her, and she threw her body backward against him as an orgasm like she'd never known ripped through her.

Whispering affirmations, Paul stilled his hands, sliding them into hers before lifting their arms up and over his shoulders, then crisscrossing her wrists at the nape of his neck. His breath was coming in short spurts as he uttered in her ear, "That was so hot. I almost came watching you. I love knowing I can do that to you."

"That was incredible. I'm still vibrating," she managed into the crook of his shoulder. "But I want you inside me. Now."

He entered her from behind with a deep, throaty groan. He was motionless at first, as if savoring the intimacy. Then, placing his hands on her hips, he began to propel inside her. He grew in her, pumping faster and faster, as if his thirst for her was unquenchable. His hands slipped upward and pressing his palms against her breasts, he bore himself so deep into her soaking center that Moira had to brace herself against the hot tub or be thrown forward. She started moving with him, wanting to answer him in passion, but she felt herself start to climax again. "Oh God,"she growled into the darkness.

"Come on, baby. Come again for me. I'm about to blow."

And just as he lunged forward and emptied himself into her, Moira obliged him.

*****

"The best thing about lasagna." Paul fed Moira another bite. "Is that you can't ruin it. Even if you burn it a little."

She chewed and smiled, then disagreed with a kiss, "No, the best thing about lasagna is eating it in bed."

They were doing just that, with Moira wearing only the resort robe and Paul in the sweatpants he'd brought on a whim. The ends of her hair were wet from the hot tub, her eye makeup was long gone and her lips had been stripped of their gloss. And to Paul she'd never looked more beautiful.

"I take that back," Moira self-corrected around a swallow. "The best thing about lasagna is eating it in bed with you."

All he needed in bed was her, he thought. He already wanted her again.

She fanned a hand in the air in front of his face. "You there?"

"Sorry. I was thinking about where we should make love next." He set the plate on the nightstand and eased her back on the stack of pillows. "Maybe we should try the bed this time. It feels pretty comfortable."

Moira laughed up at him. "Then where?"

Paul was enthusiastically debating that when the sound of his phone filled the air. With an exhale of frustration, he hung his head over Moira's chest for a moment, then decided to ignore the call. "The possibilities are endless," he said. "The double shower would be interesting."

That seemed to intrigue her. Wreathing his neck, she leaned up to kiss him. "Yeah. We could get creative with the bench." She looked toward the bathroom briefly, as if constructing the scene in her mind. "Like we did in the hot tub. Not much to hold on to but—"

Chad Kroeger's gritty voice cut her off. "It's Jack," Paul informed her around an exasperated breath.

"Does my brother always call you at this hour?" Her tone was a blend of concern and irritation. "On a Sunday night no less?"

Paul found that equally as odd. "No." He rolled off of her and got out of bed, heading toward the kitchen where he'd left his phone.

Not only had he missed Jack's call, but two others as well. Momentarily, a text from him popped up. *Where are you guys? Moira isn't picking up either.*

"What's up?" Moira called.

Something, Paul realized. Not wanting to alarm her, he answered casually, "No telling. Where's your phone?"

Moira appeared at the bedroom door, tying the belt of the robe around her waist. "It's probably still in my bibs."

"I'll get it. Go back to bed. It's cold out here."

"Thanks," she said with a weak smile, but stayed where she was.

He headed for the laundry room, adjusting the thermostat on the way. Moira's ski pants were hanging on the hook next to his and he unzipped the pocket and retrieved the phone. It was on fumes but still managed to brighten the dimly lit room enough for him to see there were two missed calls from Jack. The text message icon indicated two unopened messages.

But that's as far as he got. Because the phone started ringing and Lindsay's picture popped up on the screen. His first thought was that something had happened with the baby. Jack had been trying to reach Moira on Lindsay's behalf. Or something had come up at the office; the alarm had a tendency to go off erratically on windy nights. The consecutive calls were just a coincidence. Either way it couldn't be good news. But Paul never dreamed it would be this bad.

CHAPTER SEVENTEEN

The casket disappeared, inch by slow inch at first, then faster as gravity prevailed. A sharp ratcheting sound filled the air as the shiny brown lid disappeared into the freshly dug grave. The pallbearers shed their gloves, the mourners refreshed their sympathetic smiles, the car-lined lane emptied.

And Moira stood frozen.

She felt Paul's hand resting on the small of her back. Occasionally he would move it in a soothing, circular motion, as if to remind her he was still there. But that she would never forget. Because he had been right by her side for the last five days. For some reason, she'd had a feeling something terrible was about to happen as she watched him leave the bedroom in search of his phone. When he returned a few minutes later he had her phone in one hand, his in the other and a disconsolate look on his face. And the news of death stalled on his lips.

"Lindsay?" she'd begged in a desperate whisper. "The baby?"

Approaching her cautiously, Paul shook his head from side to side.

"Thank God." But she'd only been half-relieved, knowing there had to be more.

She remembered furrowing her brow in confusion and feeling her eyes narrow as she watched him come to her. He'd put a strong arm around her shoulders and brought her to him.

"Not one of the boys!" she'd prayed out loud.

"No," he'd quickly assured her. He'd clutched her tight, pressing her face into the base of his throat for a few seconds. "It's your dad, Moirs. Paul had continued to speak, attempting to explain what had happened. But from that point on all Moira heard was a soundless, monotonous babbling. She had no idea what Paul was saying, but the message was clear.

Her father had a heart attack.

While they were making dinner and laughing in the kitchen.

He'd been rushed to the hospital.

While they were making love in the hot tub.

And had died.

While they were spoon-feeding each other lasagna in bed.

"Ms. Brody, we're almost done here," came a soft-spoken voice. "Your brothers took your mother to the car." Returning to the present, Moira shifted her gaze to the portly man in a dark suit. "Take as much time as you need. Just let us know when you're ready."

Paul and the man exchanged a look of understanding. "I think we're ready," Paul told him. "We need to get to the house anyway."

With a tight nod the funeral director took his leave. Paul's hand slid down Moira's side and took hers in a supportive squeeze before they turned around and headed toward the limousine parked on the cemetery lane. They walked for a few silent paces before Moira said, "Thank you."

"You're welcome. But for what?"

She couldn't begin to tell him. "For everything. For being there."

"I've known your dad since I was a kid."

"I know."

"You would've done the same."

She nodded in wholehearted agreement. "I mean thanks for being there for *me*."

He grunted through his nose. "Why wouldn't I be?"

"I don't know. It's not like we're commit—"

"Moira!" Jack's voice came out of the near distance. They stopped walking and watched as he caught up with them. "Did they give you the burial flag? From when Dad was in the Army?"

"No. I thought Mom had it."

"Me too. She's a little confused, frazzled. She's upset because we can't seem to find it."

"It has be here somewhere, or with someone. Maybe it'll show up back at the house."

"That's what I said. But she's beside herself. Can you go talk to her? I need to find Emily and help her hand the boys over to her parents. They're going to take them home."

Moira sighed resignedly. "Okay."

"Let me help Emily with the boys," Paul immediately offered. "You two go and figure this out. Your mom is upset enough without having to worry about the flag."

Moira felt a smile sneak through the grief. Paul was so good, so solid. So like her brothers and her dad…was. "That'd be great. Thanks."

"Yeah, thanks," Jack reiterated. "Emily is meeting them in the parking lot. They're switching out the car seats. Damn things. It'd be easier to just trade cars."

"I have them. I'll meet you back at the house." He gave Moira a parting kiss, then Jack a slap on the back and headed for the parking lot.

Moira watched him leave, then fell into step with her brother. "Doing okay?" Jack asked, putting a comforting arm around her shoulders.

She leaned against him. "Yeah. It hasn't sunk in yet. It's true what they say; you're so busy at first, caught up in the arrangements, going through the motions. I guess it'll hit all of us in the next few days. Then Pat and Kevin will go back to their lives, you and I will go back to the business and Mom will have to adjust to a new normal."

"Speaking of the business, we'll need to work some things out in the coming months. Make sure Mom is taken care of financially in the long run, work out a payout over time for Pat and Kevin's share. That teardown in Incline would go a long way toward making all of that a helluva lot easier. I hope to have an answer next week."

"All right. Just let me know what I can do. I still have to place that ad for office help. It's more important now than ever."

"Emily's sister might be interested. Her youngest is in kindergarten now and she's been thinking about doing something part-time during school hours to earn extra income. We'd have to be flexible with her in case something comes up with the kids, but she'd be a trustworthy and dependable employee."

That made perfect sense to Moira. "That'd be an easy fix. Should I call her next week? I don't feel like dealing with it today."

"I'll ask Emily to talk to her about it, test the waters. I'll let you know what she says."

"Okay. Emily's really been great through all of this."

Jack's businesslike countenance broke into a huge grin. "Yeah. I don't know why I'm surprised. She always gets right in there and rolls up her sleeves, you know? No matter what's going on."

There was a momentary lull, then Moira put in, "It was good of Michelle's parents to come."

Jack's posture tensed a bit, then went ramrod straight. "They were friends for years, even before Michelle and I were a thing. Remember the New Year's Eve parties and Fourth of July picnics? Dad and Mr. Flynn used to go trout fishing together from time to time."

Moira nodded at the memory, then suggested on the fly, "Let's not worry about the flag right now. It'll turn up. Let's get Mom home for the luncheon. Lindsay is there already, greeting everyone, overseeing the food, but Mom needs to be there sooner rather than later." The wind was picking up, blowing the massed gray clouds across the sky like billowing dandelion seeds. And Moira's hair into knifelike streaks across her face. She tucked it behind her ears fruitlessly. They were approaching the limo now and slowed their pace.

"Okay, "Jack concurred with a shake of the head. "It was nice of Lindsay and Brian to handle the catering. One less thing for us to worry about."

"She feels almost as bad as we do. Dad gave her away at her wedding for God's sake. She was like his second daughter. And she understands. Now that I'm going through it, I wish I would have been there for her more when her grandmother died."

"What are you talking about? You were. We all were."

"You think you are until it happens to you and you realize you really couldn't be, not all the way at least. Sharing someone's grief isn't the same as experiencing your own. Then you understand."

Jack shrugged. "That's not your fault. You wouldn't wish it on anyone, but it happens to all of us eventually in one way or another. Lindsay knows that. Paul, too. He's really been there for both of us."

"He loved Dad too, like an uncle or something."

"I know." They stopped walking and Jack turned to her, saying, "I also know that you've been staying with Mom all week. Promise me you'll go home tonight, sleep in your own bed. I can take a turn. Pat and Kevin are staying there anyway."

"No." Moira shook her head from side to side. "You have a family to go home to. And you guys staying at the house isn't the same as me sleeping in the same bed with Mom. I don't want her to feel so alone."

"She'll have to sooner or later. She's strong enough. And Emily's parents will keep the boys overnight."

"Then it's a perfect opportunity for you to go home and spend some quality time with your wife. She'll help you heal."

"We'll all help each other heal." He put firm hands on her shoulders. "Go home tonight, Moira. I have a feeling someone will be there waiting for you."

*****

Later that afternoon, when the last of the guests had left the Brody's house and the remains of the reception had been put away, Paul walked his parents to their car before going to his own. He'd told them about the evolution of his and Moira's relationship earlier in the week over dinner, but seeing them together that way was still probably a little strange.

"Let us know if there's anything else we can do, honey," Theresa Webster said. "I'll call Kathleen in a few days to check on her."

"That'd be nice. I know she'd appreciate it."

"We're so proud of you, son," Paul Sr. added. "I know how much your support means to them, especially Jack. He mentioned more than once how you availed yourself all week."

"John was like a second father to me when I was growing up. And now that Moira and I are...," his voice faltered, "together, I wanted to help out however I could."

"And we couldn't be happier about that," Theresa told him. "I'd wondered off and on about it over the years. I always thought there was something there between you two, especially on her part."

He really was the last to know. "You did?"

"Call it mother's intuition. A sparkle in the eyes, a stolen glance here and there, like kindred spirits smoldering, not quite ready to ignite. I wasn't sure if either one of you saw it, felt it, but it was there, lingering. It just wasn't your time until now." His mother was beaming at him and she had a hint of tears in her brown eyes. "The sizzle that was missing between you and Lindsay and every other girl you've ever introduced us to. You and Moira have it. Cherish it."

173

There hadn't been that many women in his life, but Paul got the point. "I intend to. I can't believe how much time I've wasted."

"You haven't wasted a second," his mother corrected him. "Things happen when they're supposed to."

"Thanks, Mom." He hugged his mother, then shook his father's hand and said goodbye. As they pulled away, he thought how lucky he was to have been raised by them. That they were still together and solid, his father successful professionally as well as personally, his mother giving of her time and good fortune. And even though his sister was five years older and lived in Phoenix, they'd gotten along well enough growing up. He'd always known he'd wanted that kind of marriage and family, expected it in fact. And had managed to convince himself that he'd found it with Lindsay. But the way he'd felt about her didn't even scratch the surface compared to how he felt about Moira. Not only did they have their entire lives in common, she was almost like an extension of him. They were like-minded, yet different enough to complement and challenge each other. And he'd never been so attracted to a woman before. He'd ached for her this week, not only in the physical sense, but just to have her in his proximity. The smell of her, the feel of her, the sound of her steady breathing in his ear at night. He missed everything about her and the way he felt when he was with her.

He assumed she felt the same way, at least to some degree. Maybe not as consciously right now, with so much on her mind and grief in her heart. But she'd started to say something before Jack interrupted them at the cemetery that had bothered him all afternoon. He'd learned the hard way what happened when he ignored his gut in the past and he had a helluva lot more at stake here. When the time was right, he'd ask her about it. But not now. Now he'd go home and grab a change of clothes and do what he'd been doing for the last few nights to try to fill the void.

By the time he got to Moira's house it was dusk. He grabbed her mail and added it to the stack on the desk in the kitchen. He turned on the TV, hoping to catch some golf highlights from earlier in the day. He wasn't hungry after the spread at the Brody's, so he grabbed a beer and his laptop and sat on the couch to check his email. He'd told Pickett he wouldn't be in Portland this week, due to a death the family, so at least that monkey was temporarily off his back. The couple with the teardown in Incline, the lead Jack had given him, had seen his website and wanted to schedule a meeting. He responded, suggesting a day and time. Scrolling down, he skimmed over an introductory email from a real estate agent in Portland. William Pickett had passed along his contact information and she would like to schedule a time to show him some properties. Paul ran a circumspect hand through his hair. He'd ignore that one for now. He dealt with the rest of the day's messages and was debating getting another beer when he heard something in the garage. Had he forgotten to shut the door? He was heading to check it out when the laundry room door flew open and Moira appeared on the other side, still in her black dress and heels from the funeral. She held his wondered gape for a long moment, then met him halfway across the kitchen and fell into his arms. She didn't seem at all surprised to find him in her house drinking a beer.

"Hi." Her voice was watery.

"Hi," he whispered into her hair. They hugged each other so tightly that they swayed in place. Finally he shifted out of her embrace just enough to meet her gaze. Her eyes were bloodshot and the shadows under them reminded him of how she'd looked at the hospital in San Francisco when Lindsay had gotten in the accident. She seemed to have hit the wall in the hours since he'd left her at her mother's house. "Do you need something? I could have brought it over."

"Yeah." Her eyes filled with tears. "You." She laid her head on his shoulder and sighed blissfully. "This."

He kissed the top of her head. "You don't seem surprised to find me here."

"I was hoping you'd be here."

"You were?"

"That's why I came home." She hugged him again, as if making up for lost time.

"What about your mom?"

"Pat and Kevin are there. She's beyond exhausted and should sleep just fine. She and Jack insisted I come home and do the same." Moira lifted her head and covered his mouth with hers, then rested her forehead against his. "I've missed you so much."

"You have no idea how much I've missed you."

"Thank you again for being there for me. I couldn't have gotten through this without you."

"Where else would I be?" He met her weary eyes again and couldn't stop himself from picking up from where they'd left off at the cemetery. "Is this more of what you started to say earlier?"

She gave him a confused frown, only adding to her look of exhaustion. "Today was kind of a blur. What did I say again?"

"When Jack interrupted us at the cemetery. You were thanking me needlessly for the hundredth time and then started to say something about us. Something about us not being committed." He stepped out of her embrace and started to pace around the kitchen. "Because in my mind we are committed, if that's where you were going with that."

"You know what I mean. Where you'd feel obligated."

Paul instantly stopped walking. "I don't feel obligated," he stated in an even tone. "Not in the least. Actually, I feel guilty." He waved a frustrated hand in the air. "Do you know what I feel guilty about?"

"No," she answered, pressing two fingers to each temple. The question was clearly rhetorical.

"Wanting you," he self-condemned. "Wanting you so damn much it hurts. Wanting you in my arms on Sunday night because I'd slept next to you, with you, on you, for the last few nights. Wanting you to come home instead of staying at your mom's. So I finally came here in the middle of the night! Just to feel close to you!"

"Paul—"

He didn't give her a chance to get a word in edgewise, just continued his diatribe. "That's right! I've been sleeping here! Every night! In your bed! That's how selfish and self-centered I am!" He turned on his heel, took two steps away, then faced her again. "I wanted to make love to you the night after your father died! Even though I'd made love to you the night before *while* he was dying! That has to be the most morbid thing I've ever heard!"

She ran to him and threw her arms around his neck. "It's the most wonderful thing I've ever heard. Other than you telling me that you love me."

"I do, Moira. I know I do." He wanted to say he always would, but he swallowed it. That was for better, happier times. "So I am committed to you. In every way."

She looked deeply into his eyes. "Show me."

Paul felt that stirring inside him again, that inexplicable feeling consume him. Desire mixed with something else, something intangible, something bigger than himself, bigger than her, even bigger than the two of them together. Something that would never leave him, it would be a constant in his life now. But that too was for another time. "But you just lost—"

"I know," she interrupted. "It's okay. I need you in that way, too."

He responded by lifting her up and carrying her to the bedroom. He put her down on the bed and got out of his clothes, helped her out of hers. Then he loved her slowly, gently, tenderly. This was a passion like he'd never known, sweeping and strong, yet reverent and yielding. And when it was over, she laid against him, her arm strewn across his chest, and drifted off to sleep. Paul stared at the ceiling for the better part of an hour, his thoughts ruminating. He could never leave her here, even temporarily, and move to Portland. She could never go, especially now. He had to get out of this deal without ruining his professional reputation and looking like a complete ass.

He started to get up, but she tightened her grip, muttering, "Don't go."

"I'm not. I'm going to check the doors and turn off the lights." Kissing her forehead, he got out of bed, grabbed his jeans and headed for the kitchen. He locked the doors, adjusted the lights. Then he stared out the window into the night for a while. They would likely live here, at first at least. He loved this house almost as much as Moira did. They could always add-on eventually or move. He'd had a house in his head for a couple of years that had never fit any of his clients' needs. Then a realization suddenly came over him. It would be their house, it always was. He'd draw it out for her and they could tweak it to her liking. He'd sell his place but keep the club membership for entertaining and golf. Feeling a little more in control with having the beginnings of a plan, he went back to bed and slid in beside her. She was on her back now, sleeping soundly, wearing only the diamond studs he'd given her for Valentine's Day. He brought her to him and tucked the covers tighter around her. She settled against him with a contented sigh. This was home, he thought, feeling his eyes get heavy. She was home. The only place he could ever be.

CHAPTER EIGHTEEN

The next two weeks were a surreal blur, with Jack and Moira in the office doing damage control and adjusting to their own new normal. It had been one thing for Dad to step away from the day-to-day running of things after his first heart attack, but his being gone was another thing altogether. Not only were they still personally reeling from the loss, but current and future clients had to be reassured that Jack and Moira would not only carry on in John Brody's absence, but uphold the high standards for which Brody and Sons was known. Moira could see the weight of that burden resting squarely on her brother's shoulders. The only thing keeping him from losing his mind was that they'd secured the Incline job. It was a double-edged sword; great for business, present and future, but would require a lot of scrambling to get materials and subcontractors in place in a short amount of time. Then it would be hurry up and wait. It seemed everything at the lake ended up on Tahoe time.

"More? I thought we were done with all of that," Jack said, nodding toward the flower arrangement that had just been delivered.

Moira's mild gaze met her brother's defeated one. "Guess not." She shook the envelope in the air in front of her. "Do you want to do the honors?"

Despite the best intentions, flowers served as a constant, painful reminder of their father's death.

"It's your turn. Besides, I'm running up to Incline. Going to sit in on some city meeting and look interested."

"Fine," Moira acquiesced, throwing the envelope down on the front counter. "I'll open it later. Maybe donate them to a nursing home or the hospital this time."

Jack let out a decisive breath. "Dad would have expected us to keep going, Moirs."

"I know. He'd be so proud of you and how you're handling everything."

"Right back at you. Lauren starting next week will help. Has Paul heard back about his design submission on the teardown?"

"Yeah. They had a few notes, asked for a few adjustments here and there, but he has a good feeling. He's in Portland for a few days. I think they're meeting again when he gets back. Hopefully to finalize things."

"Great," Jack said, grabbing his keys off his desk. "I'll be back later." He bid her goodbye and went out the back.

Moira hadn't even settled in at her desk when she heard the front door chimes ring. She looked up, expecting to see Rodney, the delivery man, or the guy who comes around selling sandwiches to the complex businesses at lunchtime. Instead she found her brother's former girlfriend standing in front of her. Moira took off her blue light glasses and sat up straight in her chair. "Michelle."

"Hey," Michelle greeted from the threshold of the door with a timid smile. She seemed to be debating going any farther so Moira stood and approached her beckoningly.

"Come in. Jack just left."

"I know," she replied through a nervous laugh. "I was waiting in the car, figuring he'd go to lunch soon."

"Actually, he went up to the lake. We're doing a teardown in Incline."

"Wow. Way to move the needle. That'll keep you guys busy." Clearing her throat, she reached into her enormous designer bag and produced an envelope. "I'm so sorry about your dad. I had a Mass said for him." She handed the envelope to Moira. "Would you give it to your mom?"

"Sure." Moira studied the cream-colored envelope with her mother's name written across it for a moment, then suggested, "Or you could give it to her yourself. I know she'd like to see you."

Michelle took in some air, blew it out. "I'm not sure when I can get over there," she begged off. "I don't want too much time to pass."

Moira couldn't blame her. "Okay. Thanks."

"I'm sorry I missed the funeral. I didn't want to be a distraction."

"No problem. And you wouldn't have been. It was nice of your parents to come."

"Of course. They were friends for years."

Her eyes scanned the office as if looking for something to say. "So you guys are all settled in over here, huh?"

"It's been four years, so yeah."

That seemed to shock her. "Has it?"

Nodding, Moira gestured toward the chair next to her desk. "Would you like to sit down?"

She considered the offer briefly, then decided out loud, "No, thanks. I can't stay. I have a lunch appointment at one."

"Still selling pharmaceuticals?"

"Yeah," she affirmed around a short breath. "Alzheimer's drugs. Unfortunately business is booming." She paused, then added, "Moira, I also wanted to apologize about that night at Big Water. Sometimes Sarah can take things too far. I swear she forgets we aren't in high school anymore. The conversation got away from me."

Moira waved that away. "Don't be silly. A lot has happened between then and now." That was an understatement if ever there was one, she thought to herself. "A lot of much more important things."

"Yeah," Michelle agreed, "but still." She looked away again and her gaze fell on the Brody family picture on the wall. Moira suspected Michelle was thinking the same thing she was. That she could have been in it.

Just then sounds of entry arose from the back followed by Jack's approaching voice. "Moira, have you seen my phone? I was charging it somewh—"

Moira could only look on helplessly as Michelle turned ghostly white and Jack stopped short and froze in his tracks. He stood there for a full ten seconds, seemingly paralyzed in the inertia of surprise and disbelief.

"Michelle dropped off this card for Mom," Moria hurriedly explained, breaking the awkward silence. "She had a Mass said for Dad."

Before Jack could respond, Michelle put in, "I'm so sorry about your dad, Jack. He was such a wonderful man."

Jack finally shook off the stupor. "Thank you."

Michelle was wringing her hands and the tension in the air was so thick Moira could have cut it with a knife. She decided to put everyone out of their misery. "I think I saw your phone by the microwave," she told her brother.

"Right. I was reheating my coffee."

"Some things never change," Michelle interjected with a shaky laugh.

"And some things do," Jack told her purposefully. His expression suddenly lightened and he continued, "Thanks for thinking of us." Then he turned to Moira and said, "I need to get up to Incline." He started to leave, then swung back around. "Bye, Michelle." His gaze held hers for a few compelling clicks. "It was nice to see you."

"You too," Michelle returned breathlessly as both women watched him leave.

After a few seconds, Moira said, "He's happy, Michelle."

"I know." She swallowed hard, then went on, "I'm glad. He deserves it."

"I'm sorry about your divorce," Moira said and meant it.

Michelle laughed humorlessly. "Thanks. I'm not anymore. I guess the joke's on me."

"No one's laughing."

"Oh, I think you're wrong about that," she countered cynically. "But after a storied elopement and a failed marriage, I deserve it."

"It takes a lot of moxie to come back to your hometown and start over. But just keep in mind that everyone else has gone on with their lives." Moira paused, then finished deliberately, "Moved on."

Michelle nodded solemnly. "I know. My sister has seen Jack's wife at the park a few times. Ironic, isn't it? My nephews hanging with Jack's kids? Of course she always thought her kids would play with his kids. But as cousins."

"That wasn't meant to be. And Jack belongs to someone else now."

"I'm not a homewrecker, Moira."

"No, you're not," Moira agreed. "And you couldn't be if you were. But don't make messes at home for him to clean up. You should see him with Emily and the boys. It would bring tears to your eyes. And as much as I like you, have always liked you, we can't be friends. Emily is my sister-in-law, my nephews' mother. But I care about you and want you to be happy. You were like one of us for a long time."

Michelle gave her a toothless smile. "Likewise. So you and Paul are together?"

"Yeah."

"I'm happy for you, Moira. I never would have thought it, but now that I have it makes perfect sense. You two deserve each other. You're both some of the best people I know."

"Thanks."

"You'll have to let me know if absence really does make the heart grow fonder."

"What?"

"With Paul moving to Portland. Are you guys going to alternate weekends?"

"Paul isn't moving to Portland."

"Oh has that changed? I get everything secondhand from Sarah."

Moira's stomach fell to her toes. *"Sarah?"*

"She and Paul were travel buddies for a while, both going back and forth to Portland regularly. I think they even stayed at the same hotel on occasion."

Moira wasn't sure why that bothered her so much. "I didn't realize that."

"Sarah is in sales for a boutique winery in Oregon, but didn't want to relocate. So she goes back and forth a couple of times a month." Before Moira could say anything, Michelle's phone pinged. She grabbed it out of her purse and looked at the screen. "My lunch appointment texting to say he's there early. I'd better head out."

"Thanks again for the card," Moira said, giving her a hug. "Good luck to you."

"Sure. Take care."

After she left, Moira went over to her desk, plopped down in her chair and huffed out a cleansing breath. February had started out routinely enough, then had gotten a little crazy, then wonderful, then terrible. And now, just when she was starting to get her footing back, get used to all the changes, good and bad, she'd been thrown another curve ball. And she had an unsettling, sinking feeling about this one. Along with a sneaking suspicion that Michelle's information, from of all people Sarah Worthington, was correct. And that she should have connected the dots before. It also made her wonder what else she didn't know she didn't know. Paul had offhandedly mentioned a potential merger with a company in Portland, but his relocating there had never even crossed her mind. She wondered if this was what had been bothering him lately. She made a mental note to ask Jack if Paul had ever mentioned the possibility to him. Looking around the office with a resigned sigh, her eyes landed on the yet to be dealt with delivery. She might just donate the flowers as is, without unboxing them, and send a thank you note. Tomorrow, she decided. She'd had enough of an emotional roller coaster ride for one day.

*****

Jack inhaled a deep breath, blew it out. Between going back for his phone, the lunch hour traffic and people heading up the mountain early for the weekend, he was going to be late. He was only halfway to Incline Village, he discontented, passing the sign for the Mt. Rose Ski Resort. He slowed his pace, coming upon a dozen car backup around the next curve. Seeing cars with skis strapped to their roofs reminded him of his youth and the countless days he'd spent skiing up here. First with his family, then with friends. And that only brought his mind back to Michelle.

To say he'd been shocked to see her would be an understatement. But Moira was right; Reno wasn't that big of a place and it was bound to happen sooner or later. And his father's sudden death had made it sooner rather than later. She looked good, like Paul had said. The same tall, slender, blonde Michelle he'd known for more than half his life. The only real difference he'd noticed was her eyes. They seemed lackluster, dull. And he'd sworn there'd been a hint of tears in them when his had been so briefly glued to them.

Traffic was at a standstill now, allowing him to take in his surroundings. There'd be snow up here through April this year, he thought. Now that they were coming out of the nightmare of the last few weeks and he was going to be coming up here regularly for work, they should bring the boys up again. Maybe stay overnight. Emily had fond memories of Incline Village from her college years and still had girlfriends in the area. He felt the corners of his mouth turn upward and his eyes crinkle at the edges at the prospect. Then suddenly an overwhelming, consuming, propulsive feeling came over him; he wanted to go home and see his family. The honk of a horn behind him ended his musings and he proceeded to do something completely uncharacteristic and totally impetuous. He pulled into the entrance of the resort and once the traffic thinned, turned around and headed back to Reno. There'd be another meeting next month and they'd already won the bid and started the application process anyway. His presence today was merely a gesture of good faith. Good faith that could be shown just the same next month.

Traffic was much lighter in the reverse and within twenty minutes he was back down in the foothills of the Sierras. His house was in a master planned community with homes ranging from entry-level starters to multimillion dollar mansions. It was safe and family-oriented with good schools and tidy yards. Lauren, Emily's older sister, had lived in the neighborhood for almost a decade and had nothing but good things to say about raising a family there. Jack felt a sense of pride as he pulled up to his home in one of the more modest sections. They could always upgrade as their family and equity grew, but the three bedroom ranch with the big backyard was perfect for them now.

When he walked into the house, he found Emily in the kitchen washing sippy cups. She turned, hands still in the sink, and greeted him with a smile. "Well, what are you doing home in the middle of the day?"

He kissed her on the cheek. "I wanted to see you."

"Oh, that's nice," she said, turning off the water and drying her hands on a dish towel. "Have you had lunch?"

"Yeah," Jack lied. He didn't want her to fuss over him. He took her in his arms. "Are the boys asleep?"

"Yes, worn out from playgroup this morning. It's a godsend in the winter."

"Emily, I love you."

Her eyes started to shine and she gave him a confused grin. "I love you, too. What's come over you?"

"I can't tell my wife that I love her?"

She put her arms around his neck and cocked her head to the side. "Of course you can. It's just not like you. To come home out of the blue and say things like that."

But it should be, Jack thought. He had to get better about that. "I wanted to talk to you." He took her by the hand and led her to the couch in the family room.

"All right. If you weren't so giddy, I'd be a little scared," she told him as they sat down.

Jack took her hands in his and and met her expectant gaze. "I saw Michelle today."

Emily's expression instantly fell and her posture stiffened. Looking down at their joined hands, she swallowed hard and said, "Oh."

Jack lifted her chin with his index finger, bringing her eyes back to him. "No, it's a good thing." He kissed her softly. "I love you so much. So incredibly much. Moira was right."

She smiled at the sentiment, then nonplussed, "Moira?"

"She said I had to see her."

"Michelle?"

Jack affirmed with a nod. "I've been dreading running into her ever since I heard she moved back to town."

"Oh." Her voice was small, her eyes wide. "Why?"

Jack wrapped his hands around hers again, in an effort to reassure her. "Part of me was afraid I still felt something for her." At Emily's sharp intake of breath, he elaborated hastily, "I don't. Of course I don't. But Moira said I never got the closure I needed. That I had to prove that to myself once and for all. Get that monkey off my back."

Emily was silent for a long moment, then gave him a subtle nod as her eyes filled with tears. Finally she asked, "And did you?"

"Oh, yeah. No ifs, ands or buts about it." He swept his thumbs under her damp lower lashes. "Emily, I'm so sorry."

"For what?" Panic crept into her watery eyes now.

"For ever doubting myself and how I feel. I love you so much."

"Yes, you keep saying that. Well, I'm glad you saw her if it makes you like this. But why didn't you tell me you were feeling that way?"

"I didn't want to upset you."

"You're bound to from time to time. I have faith in you, Jack. In us. I trust you. Your words and your actions. I couldn't love you as much as I do otherwise."

Jack was dumbfounded, in complete and total awe of her. He had to be the luckiest guy in the world. He took her in his arms and kissed her again, more deeply this time. Then he simply held her, feeling at peace for the first time in months.

"I wanted to talk to you about something too," she said, scooting out of his embrace. "I don't know if this is the right time but here it goes." She took an emboldening breath, exhaled and stated, "I want to have another baby."

"Me too," Jack heard himself say.

Her eyes began to shine again. "You do?"

"Yeah."

"Really?"

"Really."

She jumped joyfully back into his arms, knocking them down on the couch in the process. He looked up into her beautiful brown eyes, and feeling his heart start to melt said, "It'll be fun to get pregnant on purpose this time. How much longer will the boys sleep?"

"An hour or so. Do you have to go back to work?" she asked with a sneaky smile.

"Not anymore I don't. Let's start trying."

CHAPTER NINETEEN

Paul looked around the undeveloped office space and tried to do what he did best. But he couldn't.

"The developer would configure the space to your specifications," the real estate agent was saying from across the room. "Offices, flex space, cubicles, conference rooms, whatever fits your needs."

Paul nodded in acknowledgement.

"Of course with your architectural acumen, your design input would be welcomed."

"I would insist on that."

He walked to the window with his hands in his pockets and took in the surrounding topography. The mountains were topped with fresh snow, the river was accented by graceful bridges and forests of lush evergreens abounded. But Paul saw none of its beauty. To him it looked like a barren wasteland instead of a picturesque mountain vista.

"Mr. Pickett put this space on the top of his short list of properties for you to see," the realtor informed him. "He was quite impressed."

"I can see why," Paul agreed, shifting his gaze back to her. "It has tremendous potential."

Her bright red fingernail played hopscotch on the iPad in her hand. "Unlike the previous property, this one is available for lease or sale."

The last thing Paul wanted was to enter into a purchase agreement. "We're interested in leasing, at least initially."

"Keep in mind that commercially Portland is a buyer's market right now, especially if you have cash."

She was right and Pickett did. He could feel himself getting painted further and further into a corner. Paul let out a tired breath and turned his attention to the exposed ceiling where a spaghetti bowl of electrical wires hung among rows of industrial cage lights. In any other situation he would already be sketching a rendering in his head. But the lump in his throat had moved to his brain and stalled, preventing that usually innate process.

"At this offering, the space won't be on the market long either way."

Appreciative of the quintessential spiel, Paul gave her a closemouthed smile. She was as round as a teapot with toothpicks for legs and perfectly coiffed blonde hair that lifted up from her head as if in a perpetual breeze. And she was still talking, "If we start the ball rolling in the next week, you could take occupancy in ninety days."

Paul rubbed the back of his neck. "That's a little sooner than I expected."

"Oh?" she queried, bringing her glasses to the bridge of her nose. She consulted the iPad again. "My notes indicate midsummer as the target date, sooner if possible."

"That was our initial thinking. Things are moving a little slower than we expected," Paul lied to both of them.

"These things often do. We can always tweak the timing once the property is secured."

Yes, Paul thought. Timing is everything. And his was horribly off.

"Will you be relocating any employees from Reno?" she wanted to know.

"I have a small office staff there who will remain intact," Paul informed her. "I won't be bringing anyone with me."

Anyone.

"How about yourself?"

"Pardon?"

"You'll need a place to call home here." With a smile in her step, she joined him at the window. "Is there a Mrs. Webster?"

"No," Paul told her, looking out the window again.

"In that case, I'll look forward to working with you in that capacity as well."

When he only nodded tightly, she took a different approach. "It might not be San Francisco or Seattle," she allowed, tipping her head toward the skyline, "but Portland gives Reno a run for its money."

Not when your heart is being held captive there, he thought with an internal kick.

"Can you extend your stay into the weekend?" she was asking. "We have some fabulous residential properties I'd love to show you."

"No," Paul replied, turning to her. "I have to get back."

"Maybe next time then." She shifted her attention back to her iPad. "I'll email you a summary of what we saw today, along with a few notes. Let me know how you and Mr. Pickett would like to proceed."

"Thank you. We'll be in touch." They walked to the elevator together, then parted ways in the lobby. Paul checked the time on his phone. He had almost thirty minutes before his meeting with Pickett and his office was within close walking distance. They were supposed to hammer out the financials of the merger, narrow down the property options and finalize the business plan. He should go to a coffee shop and gather his thoughts, jot down some bullet points. But first he wanted to hear Moira's voice. The three days he'd been gone felt like three months. He hit the second to last number in his recents.

"Hey."

"Hey." He felt better already. "How are you?"

Moira let out a ragged breath. "Fine. Trying to get back into the swing of things around here. How's it going there?"

"I could say the same. I miss you."

"I miss you, too."

"My flight gets in at 9:30. Will that be too late to come over?" Paul asked, hoping he already knew the answer.

"No, of course not. I assumed you would."

"Don't wait up. I'll just slip into bed next to you."

"I'll be waiting."

Paul could hear the smile in her voice and it pleased him immensely. "I have to get to a meeting. I just wanted to hear your voice. I'll see you tonight. I love you, Moira."

"I love you, too."

Paul disconnected and stared at his phone for a moment, then took in the impressive lobby, the dings of the discordant elevators, the frenzy of hurried people coming and going. And then it hit him. He didn't want all of this; all he wanted was Moira. He wanted to wake up with her in the morning and go to bed with her at night. He wanted to come home to her at the end of the day in that old bungalow with tiny closets and creaky floorboards and sticky windows. He didn't want a fancy new office. He didn't want a mansion on a hill or a car service. Surely he and Pickett could find common ground. He couldn't have achieved the success he had without learning to compromise, exercise reason. There was no rationale for going to the trouble and expense of relocating him, moving offices and staff when technology offered remote options. If he had to spend a week or two a month in Portland, then so be it. He could catch an early flight on Mondays, a late one on Thursdays. Moira could even come with him sometimes. Paul left the building and stepped out into the midday sunshine. His enthusiasm increasing with each step, he made his way to Pickett's office. By the time he got there, he had a solid proposal in his head and a good feeling in his gut.

Both of which were quickly thwarted.

"That's a deal-breaker."

"I'm not saying never." Paul leaned forward in the chair, trying to make his position clear. "I'm saying I can't commit to relocating right now."

"We've been discussing this for over a year. My age, along with the exponential growth of the company in recent years, has dictated that I take on a partner sooner rather than later. If I could clone my younger self, I would. But since I can't, I'm offering you part ownership in my company and a succession plan and buyout arrangement that any businessman with half a brain would drool over. But I need a wholehearted commitment from you, in writing. And that includes moving here as soon as possible and setting up shop, getting to know my employees, the business community, the area. I can tell the commuting is getting to you. You look like I feel."

Paul held Pickett's hardened stare. He was an absolute fool to jeopardize this deal without a damn good reason. But he had one. "This isn't a good time for me to leave Reno."

"Has your business taken a downward turn?" Pickett's tone was a mixture of concern and suspicion. "Are finances a problem?"

"No, quite the contrary. We're practically turning down work."

"So, the problem is of a personal nature?"

"That sudden death in the family," Paul heard himself say.

"Right. Who again?"

"My girlfriend's father."

"I didn't realize you had a girlfriend."

When Paul didn't say anything, Pickett leaned back in his chair and nodded perceptively. "I see. You've met someone."

Paul didn't confirm or deny, only reiterated, "I can't leave Reno right now."

"Well, that makes more sense. A woman has you all tied up in knots. I can understand that. But when the shine wears off that penny you're going to be kicking yourself. Because I'm not going to wait around forever."

"It's not going to wear off."

"Then bring her with you," Pickett suggested gamely. "That will be the real test. See if the honeymoon period lasts."

"It's not that simple. She runs her family's business."

"Then commute for a few months with Portland as your home base. If it's meant to be she can move here eventually, when things settle down there."

Paul couldn't see Moira anywhere but Reno. And he couldn't see himself anywhere without Moira. "I don't see that happening."

"I won't pretend I'm not disappointed by your sudden change of heart. Take the next few days, the weekend, to think about it."

Paul doubted he'd need that much time. He'd all but made up his mind. But at the very least he owed Pickett the courtesy of the pretense of consideration. "I'll do that. I'll be in touch."

Both men stood and Pickett extended his hand across the desk. "I really hope this works out. For both of us."

Paul shook it. "Either way, I'm honored and humbled by the offer."

Pickett walked Paul out and sent him off with a pat on the back. He was so lost in thought that the thirty minute taxi ride to the airport felt more like a thirty second elevator ride. He got through Security and slipped back into his shoes and refilled his pockets, then picked up his bag. He looked up at the flight monitors, wondering if he could make the earlier flight. He couldn't wait to get home and see Moira. It was like a part of him was missing when he wasn't with her. The irony was that she'd been hiding in plain sight all along. But he'd been too busy looking at Lindsay to see her. He was still scolding himself for his inexcusable ignorance when a revelation came over him. It wasn't just because of Lindsay; part of him had known all along they weren't right for each other. He'd been too busy looking *for* Moira to *see* Moira. Too busy looking for a soul mate, a friend, a lover, to realize that he already had all of those things in her. Moira was the love of his life and he wasn't going to risk that for a business deal. He could never ask her to choose between him and her family, him and her business, him and the life she loved. So he wouldn't.

*****

Moira rested her elbows on the desk and rubbed her temples with her fingertips. She had a splitting headache. She'd slept poorly, tossing and turning all night, then finally getting up and going into the office early. She'd initially attributed her restless night to sleeping alone again, but she knew it had more to do with her conversation with Michelle that afternoon.

Was Paul seriously considering moving to Portland? How long had that been a possibility? And why did Sarah know about it and she didn't? Admittedly, things had gone from zero to sixty between them virtually overnight. And her father's death had left her preoccupied and distracted of late. But even before their relationship evolved, she couldn't imagine why he hadn't at least mentioned the prospect. She'd meant to bring it up to Jack earlier, but had gotten caught up in work and the day had gotten away from her. And now as she watched the crimson sun slide behind the craggily mountain peaks, she realized just how late it was. She wanted to stop by the store on her way home, maybe make something Paul could heat up later if he hadn't eaten and then freshen up.

She missed him terribly and the feeling seemed to be mutual. Their conversation earlier had been short and affecting, yet implicit and full of things left unsaid. Paul seemed to be alluding to something. Something on the tip of his tongue that he couldn't quite get out. He'd said he wanted to hear her voice, almost as if he needed to steel himself with it. But why? Whatever the reason, she had a feeling it had something to do with his business in Portland and a potential move there.

She saved her work and shut down her computer, then leaned back in the chair and took stock of the office. The flowers that arrived yesterday still sat untouched. She decided to open them, write a quick note to get it over with, maybe even donate them on her way home. She grabbed a pair of scissors and walked over to the front counter. She unwrapped the gold paper, then sliced open the long, narrow box, hoping the flowers were okay despite being confined for over twenty-four hours.

But her heart dropped the second she saw them. Because what she found wasn't funeral flowers or a decorative plant, but roses. Red roses. At least a dozen of them. She sucked in a breath, swallowed it and took a step backward. This had nothing to do with her father. Her eyes rested on the envelope that lay off to the side. She hadn't paid attention to how it was addressed before. Moira Brody. Not Brody and Sons Construction or The Brody Family or Kathleen Brody. Just Moira Brody. She opened it with shaking hands and read the florist card inside. *Always thinking of you, Your Secret Admirer* was written on it in rolling script.

She hadn't heard back from Jason Parker after declining his ski date invitation, a fact that had been lost on her with the craziness of the last few weeks. If she'd taken the time to think about it, she would've assumed he'd accepted her refusal as gracefully as she'd tried to offer it. Which he likely would have. Which is why her head now knew what her gut had been trying to tell her all along. He wasn't her secret admirer. She stared at the card in her hand for a few thoughtful beats, as if it held some hidden clue. Then she turned it over and noted the small print at the bottom. Blooms and Baskets, Portland, OR. Moira looked around unseeingly, then went back to her desk. She didn't know the hell was going on, but all paths led to Portland. She rebooted her computer and began doing what she did best. Figuring things out for herself.

CHAPTER TWENTY

Paul walked into Moira's house just after eleven o'clock. He locked the door behind him, threw his keys down on the kitchen island and ran a weary hand through his hair. He was exhausted and his professional life hung in the balance, but he was home, he thought, walking down the hall to Moira's bedroom. He didn't care if she was asleep or not. He didn't care if they made love or not. He just wanted to lay with her, hold her, smell her scent next to him.

The room was lit by the nightstand lamp on what had become his side of the bed, turned down for him. Moira was asleep on the other side and he watched the steady movement of her breathing for a few seconds, then sat down on the bed next her. He was leaning down to kiss her on the forehead when her eyes flew open. Momentarily startled, she let out a jagged breath as delight replaced the alarm in her eyes. "Hey."

"Hey." He stroked her hair and laid a gentle kiss on her lips. "Sorry. I didn't mean to wake you."

"No, I wanted to see you. I was trying to stay up."

"Go back to sleep." He started to get up, but she pulled him back to her.

"Are you okay? You look exhausted."

"Yeah. Long week."

She propped up on her elbows and gave him a concerned look. "Tell me about it."

"Tomorrow," he replied, loosening his tie and unbuttoning his shirt. Standing up, he threw them both on the chair in the corner, followed by his pants. He walked to the other side of the bed, turned out the light and slid in next to her. He gathered her in his arms and she rested her head in the crook of his shoulder. And he realized she was naked. "Hmm. Now I really wish I'd made that earlier flight."

"Me too. I've been waiting for you."

"I missed you."

"I missed you, too."

"I don't like it."

"Missing me or the fact that you do?" Moira asked.

"I don't know. Both, I guess."

"Not me. I like missing you. It would scare me if I didn't."

Maybe that was part of what was eating at him. He wasn't used to being scared. Maybe that was the price you paid for loving someone. Being scared something would happen to them, or between you and them, that would keep you apart. He responded by kissing her lovingly, then fervently, and then with all the passion surging inside him. She answered in kind and the next thing he knew, he was on top of her and she was tearing off his briefs. His hands were in her hair, on her breasts, on her buttocks, between her legs. "You shaved," he noted with reverence.

"I was expecting you. Do you like it?"

"I love it. I want it. I have since the last time I had you. After this I'll just want you again."

"Then take me." She looped her arms around his neck and pressed him, and his erection, against her. Then she looked up at him. "After all, I'm yours."

Rendered speechless, Paul could do nothing but lose himself in her heavily-lidded eyes. They were brimming with desire, full of abandon and affection, but he'd seen that before. Now he saw something else in them. The future. His future, theirs together. Tomorrow he would tell her about the deal, about Portland, about everything. But not tonight. Tonight he would let himself love her, let her love him.

"Aren't I?" she was asking, her voice hoarse, her breathing shallow, her gaze locked on his.

He snapped out of it and tightened his grip around her. "We're each other's."

"Show me."

He started with her mouth, then made his way down her throat, showering her chest and stomach with kisses before licking a silky path back to her lips. Her hand was wrapped around him now and he could feel himself hardening, throbbing, oozing. She, too, was starting to unravel, arching under him as he ran his hands up and down her body, wanting to touch all of her at once. He settled them between her thighs and thrust two fingers inside her. He could feel her need building, only fueling his own. He loved knowing he could do this to her, loved hearing her pant and moan under him, loved watching her desperation to reach the peak grow with his. The uneasiness of those first few times was gone now, replaced by anticipation and longing. They began to grind on each other, increasing the pace, aching for that release only the other could provide. And just when he thought he could wait no longer, she opened her thighs and slid him inside her. She was wet and warm and teetering on the brink of orgasm. Paul was so aroused that he had to take a moment to collect himself for fear of taking her too hard. But she made quick work of that notion by lifting her hips and beginning to move beneath him, digging her heels into the mattress for ballast. He rode her, trying to keep himself in check, yet giving her all of him, as her low growls of pleasure filled the sultry air between them. Something indistinct escaped his lips just before he covered her mouth with his and the climax ripped through him, claiming them both.

*****

She had to tell him. After the way he'd loved her last night it would be criminal not to. Moira was barely on her second sip of coffee, but Paul was dressed and practically out of the house at 7:00 a.m., his mind full of business. "I need to talk to you about something before you go," she said from across the kitchen as he grabbed his keys off the island.

He stilled his hands and furrowed his brow. "Okay."

Meeting his wary gaze, Moira cleared her throat, then spit out, "I got flowers at work yesterday." She walked over to her purse and retrieved the florist card, then handed it to him. "Red roses."

He snatched it from her and read it, then looked at her through narrowed eyes. "You're just now telling me?"

"I was going to tell you last night. But I got a little...distracted."

He didn't acknowledge the excuse, but she saw a smile tug at the corners of this mouth before he foiled it. "I thought you made it clear to that joker you weren't interested."

"Me too," Moira replied mildly. "I never heard back from him. I assumed he got the message."

Paul crumpled the card, then threw it down on the counter. "Guess not."

If Moira didn't have so much on her mind, she might actually have enjoyed this. "Paul, we're not even sure it's Jason."

"Who the hell else could it be?"

"I don't know. But like I said before, playing games like this seems out of character for him. What does he have to gain by it?"

"Competition is competition. It brings out the best and worst in us. He's a salesman for God's sake," Paul answered evenly.

"Why would he send me flowers now, after weeks have gone by? And not respond to my email? It doesn't make any sense."

He only nodded discerningly at the reasoning, not giving it just due.

"And," she picked up the card, smoothed it out and gave it back to him, "they came from a flower shop in Portland."

"Portland?" he repeated incredulously, noting the logo on the back.

"They were in a box instead of a vase; each stem had a small water vial attached to it. At first I assumed they were belated sympathy flowers. I didn't even open them the day they arrived."

Paul nodded again, more begrudgingly this time, then scanned the kitchen. "Where are they?"

"At the office."

"Did you tell Jack?"

"No. He was gone by the time I opened them. And I wanted to talk to you first." She watched as Paul grabbed his phone and started scrolling. And decided to kill two birds with one stone. "Do you know of it?"

"What?" he said without looking up.

"Since you've been spending so much time in Portland. I thought you might know of the florist," she asked him in a measured tone.

Paul met her loaded stare head-on. "No." His voice was level. "I don't."

"You sure?"

He stood up a little straighter, stuck his phone in his pocket and crossed his arms over his chest. "Moira, do you have something to say?"

Moira felt his eyes on her as she grabbed the papers she'd printed out last night before leaving the office. "It's odd, don't you think? That the chocolates and flowers were sent anonymously from a city I've never been to, a city where I don't know anyone, but where you've spent the last year traveling to on a regular basis."

Paul didn't say anything, just shifted a little in place and held her steady gaze. "That, along with an inadvertent comment from a mutual acquaintance, struck me as extremely coincidental. So I did a little research. I came across an interesting article about a CEO named William Pickett. He founded an architectural engineering firm in Portland forty years ago with a thousand dollars he borrowed from his uncle. Timing is, as they say, everything. The population of the West was exploding and he tapped into the track housing, suburban sprawl, single-family home craze. He made his first million within ten years. Then he started designing schools and churches and office buildings to go along with all those houses. He grew it into a billion dollar company."

She flipped over the first page and continued summarizing from the second. "This man, a widower by now, has no sons, no heirs interested in taking over the business, no employee he's groomed to pass it on to in his old age. He doesn't want to sell his life's work to a huge conglomerate, but to someone who will appreciate it, complement it, grow it, while upholding its stellar reputation. Then one day, fate intervened and he came across a young entrepreneur who reminded him of himself. He approached him with a merger and succession proposition last year." She shifted her gaze to Paul. His expression reminded her of Valentine's Day when he'd stumbled upon she and Jason having dinner. But instead of etched in shock, his face was blank with guilt. Taking a sip of coffee, she returned to the matter at hand. "Quote: 'We are close to finalizing an agreement. I'm looking forward to spending the winters in Maui and the summers in one of my favorite places, Lake Tahoe. That's how I came across Paul Webster. Webster is a respected architect and businessman in his own right. He has garnered contracts for commercial and residential projects big and small in the best and worst of economic times. I couldn't have handpicked a better successor.' End quote."

"Moira—"

"Upon further investigation," she ignored him and went on neatly, "I found out that papers have been filed in Multnomah County to create a corporation, Pickett-Webster Architectural Engineering and Design, an Oregon company, headquartered in Portland." She folded the papers in half and ran her forefinger and thumb back and forth over the crease a few times. Then she looked him straight in the eye. "Why didn't you tell me?"

"I was going to but…" Paul ran a helpless hand through his hair. "It doesn't matter now anyway. There's nothing to tell." He managed to keep his expression passive, but she could hear the nervousness in his voice.

"Not from where I'm sitting."

"The deal fell through."

"Why?"

"It's not the right time."

"Because?"

"Because I'm too busy running my business to take on his."

Moira made a disqualifying buzzing sound with her mouth. "Try again."

"Fine," Paul acquiesced through a resigned sigh. "Because when I started this whole thing, I wasn't madly in love with you. At least I didn't know I was. It's a moot point now anyway. I'm not relocating and that was one of the terms of the agreement." Paul's tone was laced with disappointment, but he tried to hide it by finishing on a high note, "I'm sure there'll be someone else chomping at the bit to take over."

"Like you are."

"At first, maybe. But the more I thought about it, the more I realized it wasn't a good idea."

"Because?" she drawled.

"Because I like my life here and I don't want to change it."

Moira sighed internally. Men could be so much work. "Because of me?" she asked flatly, having no choice but to force his hand.

"Yes, because of you!" He waved an exasperated hand in the air.

"Why?"

"Oh, I don't know!" His tone was unapologetically sarcastic. "Maybe because every time I kiss you, I feel like it's been a lifetime since the last time I kissed you, even if it's only been a few hours. Or because when I hold you again, I feel like it's been an eternity instead of a night or two!" He came to her and gripped her upper arms. "But mostly it's because when I make love to you, I start to breathe again for the first since the last time I made love to you. That's why!"

"And what makes you think it's any different for me?"

Clearly bewildered, he simply gawked at her, gape-mouthed.

"Love isn't free, Paul. It comes with responsibility, sacrifice, commitment. If you loved me the way I love you, you'd know that."

That did it. He dropped his arms and slapped his hands against his thighs in stupefaction. "How can you say that? I'm turning down—"

"The opportunity of a lifetime," she cut him off. "I know. But if you loved me the way I love you, you'd know that you don't have to. You'd know that I'd go anywhere, do anything for you, with you, on a moment's notice."

"But your family, your business, your life is here," he astonished.

"Yes," Moira agreed with a shake of the head, "that's right. And until recently that would have been enough. But that was before I let myself love you. Before I realized what I've been missing. Before I realized I'd rather watch paint dry with you than go skiing with a window salesman. That I'd rather eat black olives from you than gourmet chocolate from a secret admirer. That I'd rather get a dandelion from you than roses from anybody else."

"Moira—"

"Is this what's been bothering you lately?" she barreled over him. "Thinking you'd have to choose?"

"Moira—" he tried again.

But she was far from done. "I heard what you said under your breath when we were making love last night."

Paul narrowed his eyes and looked away, as if searching his memory. Then he retuned to her with a confused grimace.

"I don't think you meant to say it out loud. About wanting to be my first, last and only lover. I thought it was the heat of the moment talking." Eyes holding his, she took an overdue breath and challenged, "So if you meant it, say it again."

He quickly closed the small space between them and grasped her face in his hands. "Moira, I want to be your first, last and only lover," Paul said without a moment's hesitation. "And that's completely unrealistic," he finished dejectedly.

She held his doleful gaze. "Not for me it isn't. Because I want you to be my first, last and only lover."

He looked so fiercely into her eyes, she felt the power of his stare burn in the center of her soul. "I believe that you believe that. But how many women are satisfied with one sexual partner for life?"

"I have no idea, but I know I would be as long as it's you. What more could I want than for the person I've loved for so long to love me back? I can't do anything about being your first, but two out of three ain't bad."

"What if that's just your heart talking? I don't want to rush you. I'm all but asking you to marry me."

"And I'm all but saying yes. All you have to do is ask." She paused, then finished facetiously, "Unless you're not sure it's not just your heart talking."

He answered that for both of them by kissing her slowly, deeply, poignantly, then resting this forehead against hers. "You'd really drop your life and move away with me? Just like that?"

"Well, I'd like to come back to visit every once in a while," she told him easily. "Is it too late?"

"For the merger?" He tilted his head back and shook it from side to side. "No."

"Do you want it?"

"I want *you.*"

"You have me. Do you want it?"

"As long as I have you, I think I still want it."

"Then go get it. Now, is there anything else you're not telling me?"

"No," Paul attested. "But who was it? Who made the comment that tipped you off?"

She pulled out of his embrace. "Michelle."

"Michelle?" he repeated with a frown.

"She came by the office to pay her respects. Apparently Sarah told her you were moving to Portland." Paul didn't seem as surprised by that as Moira would have liked. She decided that was for another day, though. They'd had enough drama for one morning.

"I was running into her at the airport from time to time. I must have mentioned the possibility," Paul allowed, a little nervous again, then changed the subject. "Okay, one problem solved. But we still need to figure out who your secret admirer is."

Moira nodded in agreement. "Could it be someone who wants to cause problems between us? Does William Pickett know why you had a change of heart?"

Paul waved the idea away. "Yeah, but only as of yesterday. He doesn't even know your name, let alone where you work. And he's a straight shooter. He wouldn't do something surreptitious like this. My money is still on Window Man."

Moira let out a conspicuous breath. "Paul, we can't ignore the Portland connection. Is there anyone who wouldn't want the merger to go through?"

"Not that I know of. I don't think Pickett has approached anyone else." Paul was silent for a long moment, then said, "I'll call the florist, see if they're more forthcoming than the bakery was. You get Jack's take on it. Oh, shit," he finished with a grunt.

"Now what?" She was barely out of bed and already exhausted.

"I just thought of something. I'm going to have to ask Jack for your hand. He's probably going to make me grovel just to entertain himself."

Moira smiled at the thought. "He just might. Good thing I'm worth it," she told him with a kiss.

CHAPTER TWENTY-ONE

"Thank you. I'll be expecting a call back from the manager," Paul said, then disconnected. Blooms and Baskets had been marginally more helpful than the bakery. At least they were willing to consider sharing the customer's information. As if making the biggest decision of his career wasn't enough, this secret admirer thing was really gnawing at him. He was done screwing around with Window Man or whoever the hell else was doing this. He could tell it was starting to bother Moira too. She'd taken the chocolates with a grain of salt, but a dozen red roses? The situation was escalating. He made a mental note to call Jack later. They needed a plan.

He tossed the phone down on the desk and watched it spin to a winding halt. He had to give it to Moira, he thought with a smile, she was thorough. And like a dog with a bone when she wanted to figure something out. But how odd that Sarah remembered he was considering moving to Portland and then mentioned it to Michelle. There was the time they'd both gotten grounded there, had to stay the night at an airport hotel. They ended up having dinner together, started drinking. He'd walked her back to her room and she made a pass at him, invited him in. He and Lindsay were over and he and Moira were whatever they were pretending to be or not be, but he had still declined. He didn't take advantage of drunk women and he didn't find Sarah attractive, mostly due to her haughtiness. But she hadn't taken no for an answer and he'd had to help her into her room to avoid making a scene in the hallway. She'd interpreted his gentlemanly gesture the wrong way and had all but thrown herself at him. He'd left hoping she wouldn't remember much about the evening to save herself the embarrassment and him the awkwardness when they occasionally ran into each other, like they had at Big Water. He'd been on the first flight out the next morning, but Sarah was nowhere to be found, likely sleeping it off.

One problem dealt with momentarily, he moved on to the second issue of the day and turned his attention to the operating agreement he'd spent the better part of a year negotiating. He knew the offer was still on the table; William Pickett was a man of his word. But he was also smart enough to have a contingency plan. Paul let out a reflective breath. He still couldn't believe Moira was willing to leave her family, her business, the only life she'd ever known, to move to a place she'd never even been to for him. And that brought him to another matter. He needed a ring. He'd reset his grandmother's diamond for Lindsay and had given it back to his mother after Lindsay returned it. He was the only grandson on that side of the family, so the tradition would end with him unless he gave it to his wife.

But he couldn't expect Moira to wear a ring made for another woman, even if she was her best friend. Besides, despite finishing each other's sentences, Moira and Lindsay had completely different taste when it came to such things. He could ask the jeweler to start over, use the original stone as the focal point, and create an entirely new piece. But would that be enough? He wanted Moira to wear that ring and feel special, know it was hers just as much as he was and vice versa.

He forced his mind back to the matter at hand. His lawyer had pointed out some details that needed clarification, a few concerns he had about the buyout arrangement, but for the most part, the deal with clean and fair. He would be an absolute fool not to take it, especially now that he had Moira on board. He rubbed his forehead and shut his laptop, then stared out the window. Spring was coming to the Sierras and soon the wildflowers would turn the meadows into a riot of purples, yellows and reds. The days were getting longer and spring skiing was in full swing. Even the hiking trails that had been buried under the snowpack were passable again.It was probably one of the few places on earth where you could ski in the morning and play golf in the afternoon. And he was lucky enough to live here.

So why the hell would he want to move? He had a thriving business here, his family, his friends. So did Moira. She was fine with moving now, said it would be their own little adventure, but what if she grew resentful over time? Started to really miss her family, especially once they had one of their own? They'd want their families to be involved with their children. And what would Jack do without Moira? He couldn't run the business and work the business all by himself.

What did Portland and Pickett have to offer that he didn't already have here? Did he really want to work with a bunch of people he didn't know? People he didn't trust and whose trust he would have to earn? No, he wanted to work with guys like Jack who had his back instead of someone who might stab him in the back. He wanted to design homes in Reno and Tahoe for people to live in, not industrial buildings in Portland for people to work in. He wanted to ski Squaw Valley with Moira and swim at Sand Harbor with Moira and make love to Moira on the beach in the moonlight. And he wanted to marry Moira and raise a family with her here, in the place where they'd grown up together. Paul stared at the hard copy of the agreement on his desk for a long moment. Then he picked up his phone, pulled up Google and booked a flight.

*****

"Guess what I found out yesterday?" Jack asked by way of greeting.

Moira snickered under her breath at the irony of the question. She kept her eyes peeled on the spreadsheet in front of her. "Hmm?"

"Jason Parker won't be calling on us anymore. He got fired."

That got her attention. She shifted her gaze up to his. "You're kidding."

Jack shook his head from side to side and threw his keys on his desk. "The company was bought out. They brought in their own sales force."

"When?"

"A few weeks ago. No wonder he never returned my call. He probably lost his phone when he lost his job."

And his computer and emails, Moira silently added.

"So I guess we'll never know if he was your secret admirer or not."

Moira sat back in her chair and bit the end piece of her glasses in contemplation, then said, "Speaking of that, those flowers we got the other day weren't for Dad."

Now she had Jack's attention. "They weren't?" he asked, approaching her desk.

"No. They were for me." She reached into her purse and handed him the wrinkled florist's card. "A dozen red roses."

Jack read it, then meet her eyes again. "This guy is starting to piss me off," he said in a hardened voice.

"You're not the only one. Turn the card over. Look at the florist's address."

Jack obliged, then returned to her with a puzzled expression. "Portland?"

Moira nodded affirmatively. "I don't know a soul in Portland. We have no business affiliations there. The only connection I have to Portland is Paul."

"If Paul weren't Paul…"

"I know," Moira finished for him, reading his mind. "If Paul weren't Paul, I'd say something fishy was going on there. He's going to call the florist this morning, try to get some information."

Jack nodded perceptively, then told her, "I don't like this, Moira. Not one bit. You're here alone half the time, sometimes all day. And the deliveries have been coming here."

"The whole thing annoys and intrigues me more than it scares me. It has to have something to do with Paul, though. He's the only common denominator. "

"Not necessarily. It could be a bizarre coincidence."

Moira shook her head skeptically. "Chocolates and flowers from a city I've never been to? Have no ties to? I looked up the addresses of the two vendors. They're only a few blocks apart. And not far from the office of the company Paul is considering merging with." Moira paused, then asked, "What do you know about that anyway?"

"He's played pretty close to the vest about the whole thing," Jack told her with a shrug. "At first he thought it was too good to be true. But apparently the guy is genuine. Paul is certainly deserving of the opportunity."

Moira had already decided not to tell Jack about a potential move to Portland just yet. She didn't need him freaking out right now on top of everything else.

"Speaking of opportunities, Paul is meeting with the couple about the teardown this afternoon, right?" Jack was still talking.

"Yeah, I think so. Why?"

"Landing that would do as much for his future business up at the lake as it's going to do for ours. He'd be burning the candle at both ends by going forward with a merger right now."

Moira was processing that, wondering if it would change anything, when Jack's phone started ringing in his pocket.

"Speak of the devil," he said, taking note of the screen. "Yeah." Jack listened for a few seconds, then commented, "I just heard. I agree. It's bullshit. Well, that would be difficult because he doesn't work for Sun anymore and I have no way to reach him." He listened again, then put in, "I think that's opening Pandora's box. What did you find out from the florist?" After another pause, Jack wrapped up the call. "Okay. Let me know how it goes in Incline."

"Really?" Moira said sarcastically as Jack disconnected. "I'm sitting right here."

"Do you want to be petty or do you want to get to the bottom of this?"

"I want to get to the bottom of this without being handled by the men in my life."

"Too late." Jack's face broke into a waggish grin. "Actually, it's kind of nice to have help, someone to share the load."

Moira sent him an annoyed look, but kept her eye on the ball. "What did he say?"

"He's waiting for a call back from the florist. When he found out Jason Parker doesn't work for Sun anymore, he suggested you contact him via Facebook and ask him straight-out if he's doing this. I don't think that's a good idea. And frankly, I'm no longer convinced it's him in the first place."

"Finally, *someone* is listening to reason."

"He's on his way to Incline. He'll touch base later."

"How nice of him to communicate through you."

"I have a feeling we're both going to have to get used to that," Jack said knowingly.

Moira watched him return to his desk and log on to his computer. She'd come off more nonchalantly than she actually felt about the secret admirer thing. She was more curious than anything, but it was a little unsettling. The roses made it more personal, romantic, almost possessive. She couldn't fathom who it could be. She'd had very few men in her life, and certainly no one who would do this. She'd never tried online dating and most of their male vendors, with the exception of Jason Parker, were either married or older or both and would have little to gain by pursuing her this way. She put her glasses back on and despite the uneasiness she felt inside, couldn't help but snicker to herself. Whoever was doing this had no idea what they were in for. Jack and Paul were both go-getters in their own right, but together would become a force to be reckoned with when it came to protecting her. She almost felt sorry for her secret admirer. Almost.

CHAPTER TWENTY-TWO

This was a first, Paul thought, making his way through the terminal. In the year plus he'd been traveling back and forth between Reno and Portland, he'd never done a round trip in one day. He'd also never spent the first few days of the week in Portland, gone home and then come back on Friday. But it had been worth the long day and astronomical airfare. He had to hand it to Pickett, he'd been extremely professional, a true gentleman, about the whole thing. And if Paul was being honest with himself, he'd known for a while he was going to pass on the merger. That's why he'd felt compelled to tell Pickett in person, not over the phone, that he couldn't take the deal. He'd run through a couple of scenarios in his head on the flight this morning. If Pickett took his unwillingness to relocate as an ultimatum, he'd tell him that wasn't the only thing holding him back. Agreeing to that in the beginning had been qualified on his part. Even if he and Moira hadn't gotten together, he still would have had reservations about moving. If Pickett had offered to sweeten the deal, Paul would have honestly told him it wasn't the money; his offer had been exceedingly generous. If he had tried to make him feel guilty about a wasted year of negotiations and planning, legal fees and strategizing, Paul would have said they'd laid the groundwork for his future partner and successor. But he'd said none of those things. He shook Paul's hand, praised him for having the decency to tell him in person, and wished him the best of luck in his future endeavors. And as he was walking him out of the office, also wished him a lifetime of happiness with his girl, like he'd had with his late wife, with a wise, avuncular twinkle in his eyes. Paul was thinking about that and smiling, scoping out a place to sit at his gate when he saw Sarah walking toward him. "Great," he grumbled, feeling his smile fade.

"Well, hello there." She stopped in front of him and set her carry-on down on the chair next to him, as if he'd been waiting for her. "Hanging out together at the airport. Feels like old times."

"More like old *time*," Paul corrected.

"Long day?" she asked, matching his sharp tone.

"Yes, you?"

"Long week."

"Likewise." Paul glanced at his phone and decided he had time for a beer before his flight. "Take it easy, Sarah," he said, heading for the bar across the concourse.

"Drinking alone?"

Paul turned around with a sigh. "Actually, I prefer it."

"Not me. I'm much too social. Are you on the five o'clock?"

"Yes. You?"

"Standby. Hopefully something," she finished in a tone rich in double entendre, "will loosen up."

"Good luck with that. See ya around," he told her and took his leave again.

"Has she enjoyed the gifts?"

Paul stopped dead in his tracks.

"Then again what woman doesn't like chocolates and flowers?"

Muttering an obscenity he'd never called a woman before, Paul spun around and met her smug gaze.

"I had something else in mind, but when I heard about her father I postponed it," Sarah went on arrogantly. "Such a shame. He was such a pillar in the community."

Paul clenched his fists as rage flooded this body, pounding through him like a second heartbeat. "What the hell do you have to gain by toying with Moira?"

She stared at him through gotcha eyes. "You didn't want me."

He could only glower at her, dumbfounded.

"You're the only man I've ever propositioned who has turned me down."

"What the hell does that have to do with Moira?"

"I want her to know about us."

"There was no us, Sarah."

"There almost was."

"How will chocolates and flowers prompt me to tell Moira something so incredibly insignificant?"

"Begging the question forces your hand. Your word against mine. For all she knows we slept together that night. And maybe many others. "

Paul wanted to force his hand around Sarah's neck. "And what will that prove?"

"That she got my leftovers."

"And that makes you happy?"

"Extremely."

"You're pathetic."

"I prefer efficient. The fact that Moira and Lindsay are so close, have so much in common," she paused for his benefit, "was like killing two birds with one stone. But you know how that goes."

He ignored the lightly veiled insinuation; Sarah wasn't worth his breath. "You're out of your goddamn mind! Moira isn't the leftovers, you are! I could have easily spent the night with you but I didn't." Paul was boiling inside, struggling to keep his voice level.

"Your loss. Give Moira my best." She grabbed her bag, turned on her heel and walked away.

Paul stood there for a few seconds in utter disbelief, as the anger began to fade and his pulse settled. Then shaking his head, he took the few remaining strides to the bar, sat down and ordered a whiskey. At least they knew who Moira's secret admirer was. But he wasn't looking forward to telling her how he figured it out.

*****

Moira walked into her kitchen just as her phone started ringing for what she felt was the hundredth time today. She put her purse and the take-out cartons down on the island and shrugged out of her jacket, then retrieved it. Another robocall, she vexed, then checked her messages. Paul had texted that he'd landed, but had an errand to run before coming home. She smiled at the idea that he considered this home. Suddenly melancholy, she looked around. She would miss her little house. But home would be wherever Paul was, wherever they made a life together. Always finding solace in busy hands, she put the food in the refrigerator and washed the coffee pot and cups she'd left in the sink that morning.

She owed Lindsay a call back. She'd been too busy at work to answer and had texted her to that effect. She'd replied all was well with the baby and that she and Brian would be in Incline with Kelsey at the end of the month for spring break. Mike and Delaney might come up for a weekend and she and Paul should do the same. That reminded Moira of another matter. Lindsay had begrudgingly agreed to a baby shower, but after the baby was born since they weren't finding out the sex beforehand. A weekend in Tahoe would give her the opportunity to strategize with Kelsey and Delaney about that. Surely nothing would be happening on the Portland front that soon, she conjectured, biting her bottom lip.

By the time Paul got home it would be later than usual for dinner and they'd both probably appreciate a relaxed meal in front of the TV, so she got out placemats and silverware and set the coffee table in the living room. She was debating if it was too warm to start a fire when she heard sounds of entry from the garage.

"Moira?" Paul called.

"Yeah," she answered, heading to greet him.

But he met her halfway and swept her into his arms. He kissed her so desperately, so profusely, that she lost her breath. When he finally tore his mouth away, he looked at her through eyes overflowing with emotion. "Hi."

"Hi," she heaved after a few seconds of recovery. "Wow. That was some hello."

"I missed you."

"Since this morning?"

"Yeah."

"Well, I'm happy to be missed by you. Are you hungry? I picked up Chinese."

"Yeah, but I need to talk to you first." He kissed her again, then professed, "I love you, Moira. I hope you know how much."

"If I didn't know before, I know now. It's pouring out of you. I love you, too. What's going on?"

He clasped her hand and led her to the couch, then sat them both down. "I have three things to talk to you about. I hope you'll agree I'm going to save the best for last."

"Okay." Moira could do nothing but stare at him expectantly as a strange feeling, curiosity and excitement tinged with uneasiness, gathered in her stomach. She looked on as Paul took her hands in his and blew out a bolstering breath, then rapid-fired, "Sarah Worthington is your secret admirer."

She had not seen that coming. "What?"

"You heard me. Sarah is your secret admirer."

"Why?" Moira stammered, in a state of shock.

"To get back at me. And you."

"For *what*?"

Paul started on a sigh, "Remember I mentioned that Sarah and I would run into each other at the airport occasionally?"

Moira shrugged. "Yeah."

"There was one night, months ago now, that our flight was delayed so long it would have been too late to land in Reno. We'd been drinking at the airport for a couple of hours by then. The airline put us up in a hotel. I walked her back to her room. She made a pass at me, which I declined. But she didn't take no for an answer. We ended up in her room and she threw herself at me. Before I knew it we were rolling around on the bed." The uneasiness in Moira's stomach turned portentous and usurped the excitement. She already didn't like where this was going. "I was able to take control of the situation and get myself out of there," Paul explained. "Nothing happened beyond her kissing me a couple of times." He looked deeply into her eyes. "I need you to believe that."

That would explain why Paul seemed uncomfortable around Sarah at Big Water, Moira supposed. "I do," she told him and meant it. "But what does that have to do with all this secret admirer business?"

"I saw Sarah at the airport today and long story short, she admitted to it. She did it to retaliate. Apparently I'm the first man to turn her down. And to get to you. She really does hate you and Lindsay. I owe you an apology on that. I thought you were reaching that night with the leftover comment. But she actually said that. She wanted me to feel forced to tell you about," Paul released her hands and made air quotes with his fingers, "us because it would make you feel like you got her leftovers. And because it might cause problems between us if you thought I was lying about not sleeping with her."

Moira shook her head in amazement. "That has to be the craziest thing I've ever heard. And it also explains the Portland connection, with her working there."

"Yeah." Paul gave her a weak smile, taking her hands in his again. "So you're not upset with me? For not mentioning the whole thing with Sarah before? Because other than feeling a little awkward when we ran into her at Big Water, I haven't given the incident much thought in months."

Truthfully, Moira did wish he'd told her about it before. She hated being the last to know, hated knowing Sarah felt like she had something over her. But that was girl thinking and she couldn't expect Paul to understand it. "No," she said, putting his mind at ease. "I'm glad you told me now though. And glad we know who's behind the deliveries. But I'm most glad you didn't sleep with my archenemy, even if it was before we were together."

"I think one of the reasons I didn't sleep with her was because we were together. I just didn't know it yet. So we're okay?"

Moira had to laugh. "It's going to take a lot more than a bitch who peaked in high school to cause problems between us."

"I don't want anything to cause problems between us. Which brings me to the second topic du jour."

"You said you were saving the best for last, so I assume we're heading in that direction."

"I hope so. I turned down the deal. No merger. No Portland."

She hadn't seen that one coming either. Keeping up with him was becoming a struggle. "Paul, why? Because of me?"

"No," he answered with a firm shake of the head. "Because I was talking myself into it, even with you on board. It means the world to me,

Moira, that you'd go. I still can't believe it, to be honest. You didn't even have to think about it. But we both have viable businesses here, that are only growing. Our families, our friends, our life is here. This is where I want us to make our life together. Besides, Jack would kill me. And I want my kids to grow up with Jack's kids."

"If we're on the same page, Jack's kids and your kids are going to be cousins," she reminded him gently.

"Yeah, I'm definitely on that page." He kissed her tenderly. "That brings me to the last thing I wanted to talk to you about." He took a stabilizing breath, then dove right in. "You know I had my grandmother's ring reset for Lindsay."

Suddenly that ineffable feeling was back, filling her stomach. But this time, the uneasiness was fading and the curious excitement was laced with joy. "Yes, of course."

"After our shared moment of insanity, she returned it and I gave it back to my mom. I'm the only grandson on her side of the family and the ring was traditionally passed down that way." Paul reached into his pocket and produced a small black box. "I stopped by my parents' house on my way here."

Moira sucked in a breath. "Paul."

"Hear me out." He joined their hands again. "Obviously I don't expect you to wear a ring designed for another woman, even if she is your best friend. Added to which your tastes are completely different. But, if you're okay with it, I would still like to use the diamond from my grandmother's ring. That would be the only commonality your ring would share with Lindsay's. We could go to the jeweler together and he could start from scratch to your specifications."

Was this really happening? The push and pull in her stomach melded into pure bliss now. She managed a wobbly nod.

"I stopped by Jack's after I left my parents' house. He actually wasn't that hard on me. He gave me a big hug and said he couldn't be happier. And Emily told me it was about time." The next thing she knew, Paul was down on one knee, with one hand in hers and the other holding the ring box. "Moira, I love you more than I thought possible. Will you marry me?"

"Yes, yes, yes! Of course I will!" She flew into his arms, nearly knocking them both down on the floor. "I don't care about the ring. I'd be happy with one from a gumball machine as long as it was from you."

Paul held her close for a long moment before righting them both back on the couch. "Until we can get a proper ring, would you be willing to wear this one?"

Moira looked on as he lifted the lid of the box. Inside was a small marquise-cut diamond on a plain gold band. And something about it looked vaguely familiar.

"It's my mom's," Paul informed her, reading her mind. "It was her idea for you to wear it until yours is made. My parents got engaged when my dad was in medical school; he didn't have much money. He's tried to buy her a new ring a couple of times, but she always refuses."

"Paul," she gasped, as her eyes filled with tears.

"She thought it might be a little big on you," Paul said, slipping it on her finger. "But I think it's perfect."

Moira couldn't take her eyes off of her hand. "I can't believe your mom would lend me her engagement ring."

"I don't think our families could be any happier about the whole thing." He drew her to him and kissed the top of her head. "Moira, what if I'd let you go? What if I hadn't seen what was right in front of me until it was too late?"

"I think eventually I would have somehow forced you to see me that way, to see if you felt what I did." She pulled back just enough to make eye contact. "I wouldn't have let you go without a fight," she told him, feeling the joy in her heart fill her from head to toe. "I couldn't have."

His eyes were full and dark now, not with the desire she'd seen in them so many times before, but with something else. Something sure and real and full of promise. And then she realized they were reflecting hers. "So you're okay with wearing my mom's ring for now?" Paul wanted to know. "I didn't want to wait any longer to ask you."

"Of course. I'm honored. But you knew I would be. And that I'd say yes."

"Well, I have asked you to marry me about a hundred times in my head, but this makes it official."

"You have, huh?"

"Yeah."

"And what did I say?"

"You said yes every time. It was your only option."

She laughed, then planted a kiss on his mouth and reclined against him, studying her left hand again.

"Speaking of things in my head, I've had a house in my head off and on for a few years. I couldn't understand why lately it's been more on than off."

Moira didn't know what that had to do with anything, so she took a stab in the dark. "The teardown in Incline?"

"Not quite on that level." Boosting them up a little, he reached into his pocket and pulled out a piece of paper. "I couldn't stop myself from sketching it out on the plane." He unfolded the paper and handed it to her. "What do you think?"

Moira sent him a puzzled look, then took in the drawing. It was a traditional two-story, craftsman-era house, with a wraparound front porch and cottage-style garage doors. It reminded her of a larger, more modern version of her house. "It's beautiful. But what does—" she stopped short and met his gaze as the realization struck her. "It's our house, isn't it?"

Paul nodded. "I think it always was. Welcome home, Moira."

He gathered her back into his arms and she snuggled against him. This was home. He was home. Where they'd both been all along.

SIX MONTHS LATER

On a warm autumn day, in the hills above Marin County, Delaney and Mike exchanged wedding vows. Lindsay stood next to Delaney, Brian next to Mike. And Moira stood looking on, her goddaughter Grace in her arms, with Kelsey on one side of her and Paul on the other. Her engagement ring sparked in the late afternoon sunshine and her smile was just as bright. It would be her turn soon and she still couldn't believe she could be this happy. Jack would pull double duty; give her away in their father's stead and be Paul's best man. And Lindsay, of course, would be her matron of honor. And fate would have them all where they're supposed to be. What are the *Chances* of that?

Read on for an excerpt from *Second Chance*,
Book One of the *Chances Trilogy.*

Second Chance
The Chances Trilogy Book One
By Martha O'Sullivan

CHAPTER ONE

It was only because he was here again that she kept crossing his mind. He was long over her, Brian Rembrandt reminded himself with borrowed conviction, imbibing the brisk mountain air. All he needed was a stiff drink, a thick steak and a dealer having a bad night. He wasn't much of a gambler, but the cards would occupy his ruminating mind. And no matter how tired he was, he could still count to twenty-one. Pushing down the past, he crossed the street under a cloak of pine trees draped in velvety, gray light.

He knew the way. This wasn't his first time in Lake Tahoe, especially on the Fourth of July. Summer before last, he and Lindsay had watched the fireworks illuminate the basin here before making some sparks of their own on the beach. Lindsay had always wanted to make love on the sand, when the night was still but for the aspens whispering in the breeze and the occasional swoop of a gull's wings.

Brian had been happy to indulge her. Several times.

"Good evening, sir," the hostess greeted.

"Good evening." Brian replied, stepping through the threshold of the huge mahogany doors. The ceiling-to-floor window wall gave way to a panoramic view of the lake cradled by the Sierra Nevadas. "Rembrandt for dinner."

"Yes, Mr. Rembrandt." She consulted the chart on the podium, then directed him to the lodge-style restaurant at lake level. "Right this way."

He began to oblige, but stopped midway down the stairs, momentarily mesmerized by the breathtaking fusion of pastels coaxing the crimson sun into the inky lake. So much so that when he resumed his stride, he inadvertently collided with someone. Careening on the staircase as if in slow motion, she attempted to grasp the banister for ballast.Instinctively, Brian hooked the waist of the woman half his size and pulled her to him. The force of his reach threw them both into the inside corner of the landing. "I'm so sorry!" he exclaimed, mortified.

She shook back a mane of blonde hair, revealing porcelain skin and a glossy mouth parted in surprise. And cobalt eyes that twisted Brian's stomach muscles into braided dough. He lost his breath. "Lindsay?" Her name catching in his throat, he stroked her cheek with the back of his free hand, holding her eyes in his for fear blinking would make her disappear. "My God, Lindsay." Their faces were so close together that the air her sharp breath took in had no doubt been in his lungs first.

She gaped at him, as if she'd seen a ghost, as all color drained from her face. Heart beating out of his chest, Brian gulped back the shock and righted them both, taking her hand in the process. It felt soft and damp, like a morning rose. Or maybe that was his palm sweating. After a shared moment of inertia, he asked, "Are you all right?"

She gave him a slow, affirming nod. "Brian." Her voice was barely above a whisper. "What are you doing here?" She took her hand back and lifted her chin a notch.

His gaze seemed tethered to hers. "Putting out a fire."

Brows knotting, she narrowed her eyes. "A fire?"

"Work." Brian finally shook off the stupor. "Long story."

A knowing smile curved her lips, but went no farther. "Oh."

He wondered if she meant to sound that disappointed. "I can't believe you're here. I was just thinking about you."

That seemed to surprise, then please her. Her mouth opened, but before she could articulate the thought, a man wearing a puzzled expression and a concerned frown arrived. "Linds? You okay?"

She swallowed the words, but her gaze remained fixed on his. "Yeah. I just lost my balance for a second." She paused, then added, "Paul, this is Brian Rembrandt. Brian, Paul Webster."

Brian tore himself away from her and extended his hand perfunctorily. "Nice to meet you."

Lindsay's companion met his firm handshake head-on. "Likewise."

"Are you visiting your grandmother for the holiday weekend?" Brian returned to her, biting back the urge to break the arm now girdling Lindsay's waist.

Her face clouded and her eyes hinted of tears as she shook her head from side to side. "She passed away last year."

Her irises were like bottomless pools, Brian reminded himself. And he suddenly found himself at risk of drowning. "I'm so sorry," he told her from the heart. "I know how much she meant to you."

"She did indeed." Her tone was wistful. "She was my only family."

Silence hung over them for a few steady beats. Then her companion cleared his throat and broke it in an even voice. "Our food has probably arrived by now. We should get back to our table."

Lindsay's eyes seemed to hold his a moment longer than she liked. Then she shifted her attention to her date and responded graciously, "Yes, of course. I never made it to the ladies room, though." She excused herself and started up the stairs.

Brian found himself reaching for her. "Lindsay…"

She finished taking the step, then stopped. "It was nice to see you, Brian," she tossed over her shoulder, swallowing hard. "Good luck with those fires."

Brian could do nothing but watch her walk away in stunned silence. Then his gaze drifted to Webster and a tacit message passed between them. With a superior smile and a chuckle in his eyes, the other man pivoted on his heel and retreated.

"Mr. Rembrandt?" called a voice from below. "I can seat you now."

Brian turned his head and nodded to the woman not much older than his daughter. He made quick work of the remaining stairs and fell into step beside her.

She showed him to a high-top table in the bar area. "Just one for dinner, right?" she confirmed politely, removing the second table setting.

"Yeah," Brian confirmed around a grunt. "Just one."

*****

"Where are they?" Lindsay scanned the beach. Finally, she spotted them down by the shore. The man pointed her out to the little boy, who began running toward her. "Mommy, Mommy! We found sea glass! Isn't it cool? Is it like the kind you used to find when you were little?" the towhead asked, wide-eyed with wonder. Nodding adoringly, Lindsay gave the crown of his wet head a tousle, then addressed his father. "Time for lunch." He

lifted the boy to his shoulders, then leaned down to kiss her...

Lindsay woke heaving shallow breaths. She sat up in bed with a shiver and rubbed away the goose bumps erupting on her arms. The soft breeze raised the curtains, inviting the moonlight to streak the thick planks of her bedroom floor. She got up and closed the window before sitting on the window seat and gazing into the pre-dawn darkness. She hadn't had a dream like that in ages. Seeing Brian must have triggered it.

And that had been very real.

She could still feel his hand on her cheek, she thought, raising hers to the same spot as the dream turned inward. And the rest of him looked as good as his hand had felt; the chiseled cheekbones and strong, square jawline on his perpetually suntanned face. She'd run her fingers through that ash blonde hair, slept against those broad shoulders and lost herself in those strong arms countless times. He'd smelled morning fresh like he'd just showered and was dressed casually in khaki pants and a collared shirt. He was here on business, he'd half-explained. She'd barely heard the words for the ringing in her ears and the thudding of her heart. And the hope that danced within her when he said he'd been thinking about her.

She'd been thinking about him too. But that was nothing new. She'd thought about him every day over the last year. From the day she moved out of her apartment in San Francisco to the day she buried her grandmother. And, of course, yesterday when she'd found that yellowed, rectangular-shaped box in the attic. Now it was a new day, she thought, as the first bands of light fought the charcoal dim behind the mountains and she was thinking of him still.

But that would have to change.

Soon she would be Mrs. Paul Webster, son of one of the most highly regarded oncologists on the West Coast. And his wife, philanthropist extraordinaire, credited for raising millions of dollars for the new pediatric cancer wing at Reno General Hospital. One that, coincidently, her architect son had designed. To whom Lindsay owed an apology.

She'd foregone the ladies room for fresh air while, unbeknownst to her, Paul was instructing the kitchen to box their dinner. Once home, she barely picked at her food and after exaggerating an aching head, begged off the fireworks. After Paul left, she poured herself a healthy glass of wine, sat on the upstairs deck and had a good cry as the night sky exploded with color. She'd considered calling Moira, but she would have insisted on driving up. She'd had a date last night, her first in months, and Lindsay had no intention of ruining it on the whim of a lovesick girlfriend.

She let out an acquiescent sigh and ran an equally resigned hand through her hair. Must the Mountain Chickadee be so damned chipper at this hour? From its incessant chirping you'd think it didn't have a care in the world. Envious, Lindsay grabbed her robe and went downstairs. Her bare feet cringed on the cold wood floor as she made her way to the kitchen. All was quiet on the lake. The fishermen weren't out yet, the tourists were asleep and it was too early for the locals to go about the business of life.

He'd been alone, she lightened, ladling a heaping scoop of grounds into the filter. If he was seeing someone surely she would have accompanied him here on the holiday weekend, even on short notice. Not that it mattered, she reminded herself, extending her left arm and studying her hand, soon naked no longer. The solitaire had belonged to Paul's grandmother and the smaller diamond her mother's before her. He'd added to the original stones and reset the aggregate on a traditional gold band. Down on bended knee, Paul had been distracted by the ring slipping off, sparing him the astonishment that had no doubt flashed across her face, short-lived as it had been. Because the more she thought about it, the more sense it made. She loved Paul, after all. They had all but grown up together, had the world in common, wanted the same things. He would be a loving, faithful husband and a devoted father. The coffee maker beeped, ending her incongruous flight of fancy. Doctoring her coffee, she headed upstairs to start her day. She'd chosen the dream over the man. So she might as well start living it.

CHAPTER TWO

The lake glistened like a sheet of sapphire glass reflecting the limpid sky, its silky waves swishing concertedly against the shore. The scent of suntan lotion and pine straw laced the breeze and Brian could taste summer in the air as he walked through the sand and crossed to the neighboring beach.

More gingerly than he liked, he self-admonished.

He'd relinquished his table for two and taken his dinner at the bar. Only he ate too little dinner and drank too much Scotch. Which was why his mouth felt stuffed full of cotton and his head pounded like a jackhammer.

But that's not why he'd rescheduled his flight.

He looked on as the reason he had crouched at the shore, as if searching for something in the fawn-colored sand. After a few moments of running her hands through it, she brushed them off and stood. Instantly the quicksilver of Brian's heartbeat spread to his cock and ignited. He had feasted on those voluptuous breasts, slept wrapped around those dancers' legs and unsparingly indulged himself in everything in between. And last night all he could think about was Paul Webster doing exactly the same thing. Which was why he was standing on the beach sweating his ass off instead of emptying his pockets in Security right now.

He watched as Lindsay, oblivious to his lecherous contemplation, smoothed her hair and sat down. Sparing the phone on the chaise lounge a cursory glance, she tossed it into the mesh bag at her feet. She briefly considered the magazine that lay next to it before it saw the same fate. She reclined and within seconds her breathing leveled and her breasts began to move up and down steadily inside the clingy halter top. He wondered why she had done away with her sexy belly button ring.

Brian made his way to her. He stopped just short of her chair and shrouding her in his shadow, swallowed hard and found his voice. "Lindsay."

Her eyes flew open behind the Ray Bans she wore and her lips parted in silent surprise for a few blinks. Then, in a voice colored with awe, she sat up with matching consternation. "Brian."

Holding her eyes in his, Brian decided he didn't care if she was alone or not. He was going to say his piece. "May I?"

"Sure," she stammered, gesturing to the foot of the chair and scooting up to the top. Cocking her head to the side, she took him in. "You remembered this is my beach."

He hated that she found that so shocking. "Yeah," he told her. "I remembered." He sat on the edge of the cushion, mindful to leave a buffer zone between them. She was looking at him expectantly, as if waiting for him to speak. So he did. "What happened to you last night? You disappeared."

Again.

"Yeah." She sent a revelatory look out over the water. "I had to get out of there."

Brian felt the knot in his stomach tighten. "I waited for you to come back."

Again.

Her gaze snapped back to him. "You did?"

Apparently she found that as surprising as he had. "Yeah, I did."

She seemed to struggle to remain impervious, but a hint of satisfaction crept into her eyes. "Oh."

That relaxed him a little. "How have you been? Did you get through your thesis? Finish your MBA?"

The twinkle immediately faded. "No, all of that got shelved when Gram got sick. Pancreatic cancer can be very aggressive. Then I had to settle her estate, get everything in order. I'm just now turning my attention back to school."

Brian fought the recurring urge to take her in his arms and hold her until the doleful look in her eyes went away. Instead he kept his feet planted firmly in the sand and the palms of his hands glued to his thighs. "I'm sorry you've been through such a hard time. I'm even sorrier I couldn't help you through it."

Deep emotion had settled in her eyes now. "Thanks. Moira was with me every step of the way. And Pa—" She switched gears midway. "And the Brodys collectively were great."

Brian's blood was starting to boil and it had nothing to do with the heat of the day. He clenched his teeth. "Can we go somewhere to talk?" Or dinner later, he thought but didn't dare ask. He didn't want to hear she had plans with Webster. When she didn't answer, he laid his hand on hers. "We could walk out on the pier and have a drink, watch the boats come in." He nodded toward the hotel pier a few hundred yards away. "I'm staying over there."

She considered first his face, then his hand resting on hers. "Let's talk inside instead." She swung her legs over the side of the chair and began gathering her things as if the matter had been settled. "It's time I went in anyway."

Brian nodded by way of reply and helped her up. As they fell into step together, trudging through the coarse sand, Lindsay shot him a oblique grin. "Wait until you see what I've done with the place. You won't believe your eyes."

*****

"Would you like something to drink? Beer, water, a soft drink? It's a little early for wine, but I have that too," Lindsay offered from her kitchen a few minutes later.

"I'm on the wagon today," Brian told her. "I'll take a water."

She grabbed a bottle from the refrigerator as Brian took in the kitchen. "The place looks fantastic. The frosted glass panels remind me of—"

"The place we rented in Napa," she finished for him incredulously, aware of the similarity for the first time. It was a wonder either of them remembered any room other than the bedroom in that vineyard cottage. She fastened another button on her tunic and cleared her throat. "Thanks. I wanted to maintain the vernacular feel of the house, but modernize. So I went with browns and greens, like the siding and the roof. The floors are original; I had them sanded and stained. For a darker contrast against the walls." She paused, watching Brian shift his steel blue eyes to the French doors leading out to the deck. A brilliant blue haze had settled over the basin, encompassing the lake and the mountains beyond. "But there's no competing with Mother Nature." His gaze cut back to hers and she saw the same uneasiness on his face that she felt in her stomach. "We decided to go with a peninsula instead of a table and chairs," she continued, struggling to keep her voice level. "Knocking out that area doubled the size of the kitchen."

"We?" Brian asked, shoving his hands into the pockets of his deeply creased shorts. His eyes rested on the red roses bursting from a vase on the granite island.

"Jack Brody, Moira's brother, and I. They did the remodel." Brian nodded in recollection, and she saw relief flicker in his eyes. It resurrected the guilty hope from the night before and curved the horizontal line she had planted on her mouth into an unintended smile.

They held each other impalpably for a few seconds until Brian, eyes reverting to the lake, observed, "The wind is picking up already. Tonight won't be as calm as last night." His regard returned to her and it reflected the double entendre of his words.

"No, it won't." Her stomach bit as she went to the sink and nervously began washing dishes that were already clean. She cleared her throat and tried to make conversation. "So, did you get those fires put out?"

"Temporarily." Joining her, Brian grabbed a dish towel. "Remember All Tech Software?"

"Of course. They were one of your biggest clients."

"Sacramento has a problem with the emissions from their plant near Fresno. Fresno being the breadbasket of the world, the state is particular to environmental code compliance there. The state shut them down last week," he elaborated. "We've worked out a thirty-day stay, but I'll have my work cut out for me when I get home."

Lindsay sighed inwardly, rinsing a bowl for the third time. It should feel odd to be standing with him here at the kitchen sink, doing dishes and chatting about the latest crisis at work. But it didn't. And that was a problem. She almost had to remind herself not to ask what sounded good to him for dinner or what their plans were for the weekend. Instead she changed the subject. "How's Kelsey? She graduated this spring, right? I wanted to send her something but thought it might be awkward."

"She's great, starts at USC in the fall," Brian answered with a proud smile. "And it wouldn't have been awkward. She still asks about you." He paused, then finished quietly, "She says I was a fool to let you go."

Lindsay's hands froze under the water and her breath hitched, but she willed her eyes steady, trying to remain focused on the busywork. Until Brian turned her by the shoulders and taking her face in his hands, proclaimed, "She's right." His gaze fell to her mouth and after a long, poignant beat, he brought his lips to a whisper away from hers and hovered. She found herself barely able to expel breath, let alone move. She could only close her eyes in anticipation as he grazed her lips with his. Finding no resistance, he curved a hand behind her neck and pulled her to him. He laid his lips on hers and began to move slowly over them. The familiar taste and texture of him felt like coming home after a long journey.

His mouth was hot and hungry. Very, very hungry as if it hadn't eaten in eons. And when her lips alone weren't enough to satiate it, he parted them and placed his open mouth squarely on hers and plunged his tongue deep. He fed greedily, drawing all of her into his mouth and feasting little by little, bite by bite, until not a breath remained between them. Then with a spent sigh, he ran his tongue along her top teeth so sensually that she quivered with long forgotten dampness below. "Lindsay," he mumbled her name as if he'd never said it before.

"Brian," she heaved in kind.

"I miss you." He let out a jagged breath. "I miss us."

She let the joy of basking in Brian's arms again run through her, warm her. Until she realized she was in Brian's arms again. She sprang back, mortified by her visceral reaction, and braced herself against the bank of cabinets that lined the back wall of the kitchen. She had to put some space between them. "I can't do this."

"I'm sorry." Brian's voice was thready. "I wasn't trying to—"

"Don't apologize," she managed. She saw the lust brimming in his eyes now, but it was laced with something more. Something profound. She wondered if he was seeing the same in hers. Still, she shook her head. "You need to leave."

"The hell I will. We need to talk this through."

She opened her mouth, closed it again and drew a stabilizing breath. "There's nothing more to say.

We had a wonderful year, but we want different things," she told herself as much as him.

Anger flashed across his face and crept into his eyes, replacing the vulnerability she'd seen in them. "It was a helluva lot more than a wonderful year and you know it," he countered, trudging a hand through his hair and starting to pace. "How could you just leave like that?"

Lindsay had asked herself that a million times. And the answer was always the same. She trailed him inertly. "Because I had no other choice. I had to be honest with myself. We had to be honest with each other."

"Why did it have to be all or nothing?"

"The longer it went on, the harder it would have been to let go."

"That's bullshit."

Completely unnerved now, she painted a stoic expression on her face and crossed the room. Standing her ground, she opened the door and repeated, "You need to go." Her tone was a complete contrast to the tears burning in her throat. "Please."

Brian sent her a resigned nod, then grunted in deference. "Fine. I'll go, but it's not over. Not by a long shot." Tipping her chin, he brought her gaze to his. "Because I'm not going to be able to stay away from you this time." He released her gently and walked out the door.

Shaking inside, she watched him cross the yard and take a few steps onto the sand. Then he stopped and faced her again. "Honesty, huh? I'll give you honesty. The most honest year of my life was the one I spent with you." He turned on his heel and walked down the beach in the direction of the hotel. Closing the door, she gave into her rubber-like knees and slid to the floor. She had, hundreds of times, told herself she'd done the right thing for her, for the both of them, in the long run. So why was she suddenly filled with such regret?

CHAPTER THREE

Brody and Sons Construction had relocated their office to downtown Reno a few years ago when the riverfront revitalization was in its infancy and the government incentives were too good to ignore. That worked just fine for Moira. She'd much rather be here among the boutiques and cafes than stuck in an industrial park on the outskirts of town. She did the books for the business and saw to the day-to-day running of things while her father and brothers were out in the field.

It was exactly what she'd promised herself she would never do.

She'd earned an accounting degree and wanted to be the CFO of something, anything, but Brody and Sons G.C. She wanted to live in San Francisco or L.A. or Chicago. But the housing boom had changed all of that. As had the economic downturn that followed. So she'd stayed. She'd modernized the office and computer systems, automated bill payment and increased efficiency while decreasing expenses. She'd hired and fired, wrangled with the county and even convinced her father to invest in going green. And somewhere along the way, she actually started liking it. It was the first thing she'd ever done all by herself. Something no one had taught her; she'd figured it out. Something to call her own.

Moira was alone in the office today; officially they were closed for the long holiday weekend. But Jack needed quotes run and people expect to be paid, holiday or not. If she finished early enough, she might call Lindsay and invite herself up to the lake. "It's hotter than hell down here," she muttered out loud, reworking her hair into the claw clip at the back of her head.

She didn't look up when the door chimes rang, assuming it was Jack or her dad. And they could wait until she hit send. She blew her side-swept bangs out of her eyes and turned around, momentarily unsettled by how pleasantly surprised she was to find neither one of them standing in front of her.

"Hey."

"Hey, yourself." Moira returned the greeting, pushing up from behind her desk. Paul was Moira's definition of conventionally handsome. If it wasn't his caramel-colored eyes and dark, wavy, hair, it was his olive complexion and athletic build. Was it her imagination or did he hug her longer than usual? Breaking apart, she cocked her head to the side and studied him. His face was as long as a summer day and his eyes as sullen as a scolded puppy. Her smile plunged along with her stomach. "Did something bad happen? Is Lindsay all right?"

"I don't know," Paul answered flippantly, shrugging his shoulders. "You two finish each other's sentences. You tell me." He perched himself on the edge of her desk, one denim-clad leg bent at the knee, and looked at her sharply.

Moira was a terrible liar, never one to think on her feet. She threw her glance around the office, searching for an answer. And came up empty. "I don't know what you mean."

She watched Paul cross the room and stare out the window at the waves of heat radiating off the pavement for a long moment. He was probably the only man she knew who could wear a pink polo shirt without looking the least bit feminine.

"Does Lindsay want to get married?" He started to say something else, but changed his mind and swallowed it.

"She said yes, so I assume so," Moira reasoned flatly, threading a pen through her fingers.

He spun around to face her. "Why?"

"Why what?"

"Why is she marrying me?"

Moira returned to her desk and started shuffling papers needlessly. "I guess because she loves you and wants to spend the rest of her life with you, Paul. Isn't that why people usually get married?"

He met her snarky look head-on. "Usually. But there are a host of other reasons. Convenience, financial security, procreation, companionship."

Moira watched the pain of these possibilities cross Paul's face and settle in his eyes. "Yes, I suppose there are all those reasons. But Lindsay has plenty of money, thanks to her grandmother.

She's too young to worry about her biological clock and let's face it." Moria laughed around the words. "She's beautiful and doesn't know it, making her no stranger to male companionship." He was standing right in front of her again and she could smell the anise in his cologne. It ignited every cell in her body and forced her to concentrate on drawing breaths. She started to reach out to him, but thought better of it and slapped her hands against her thighs instead, asking, "Where is all this coming from?"

"Oh, I don't know," Paul began sarcastically. "Lindsay seems to have an excuse for everything lately, especially when it comes to the wedding. She's always gardening or busy or something." Waving his hand in the air dramatically, he finished in a low growl, "And you no doubt heard who we ran into last night."

She gave him an affirming nod. There was no use in pretending otherwise.

"Part of the reason she and Rembrandt." He spit the name out like a bitter pill. "Parted ways was because he didn't want to settle down, commit. So she is worried about her clock."

Moira wished she were anywhere else. She had Paul's undivided attention and had not a stitch of makeup on and had thrown her hair up right out of the shower. She scolded herself for self-indulging and conjured up a compassionate smile. "I think you're being paranoid, but to set your mind at ease, just ask Lindsay." As the words slid off her lips, she knew they would never come to fruition. Paul was too afraid of the answer to pose the question. He'd live with a shadow of doubt rather than risk an inconvenient truth. "She probably just needs some space. Everything is happening so fast."

Gaze lingering on hers, Paul shook his head up and down contemplatively. Then he waved off whatever he was thinking and flashed her that killer smile. "I know, I know. You're right. What would I do without you, Moirs?"

The irony of the guileless statement not lost on her, Moira smiled in spite of herself. "Live a perfectly normal life."

He chuckled uneasily, as if the thought returned and startled him. Then his eyes swept the office, seeming to notice they were alone for the first time. He took a step back and cleared his throat. "Want to grab some lunch? My treat."

They'd had countless meals together over the years of course, but that was before. Before the slow, unbidden epiphany. A realization Moira had shared with no one. Whenever she let it enter her mind, dread curled up inside her. Like it was right now. She justified her silence with guilt and reason. No one deserved a guy like Paul more than Lindsay. Paul would never feel that way about her anyway. She was his best friend's sister. She would put her feelings aside and get over it. "How about a rain check? I've got a lot to do here."

"Sure." Silence hung over them for an interminable moment until a series of soft beeps filled the room. Paul shifted his gaze to the phone on Moira's desk. "Well, I'd better let you get back to it."

"Yeah," Moira agreed more hurriedly than she liked. "Duty calls."

He wagged a playful finger in the air. "I'm gonna hold you to that rain check."

"Deal."

"See ya, Moirs."

"Bye," she said and watched him walk out to the parking lot under the cloudless desert sky.

*****

"Damn it!" Lindsay said to no one and blew the errant strands of hair out of her face. Determined to put her nervous energy to good use, she'd picked up some stacking stones at the nursery. Knees bent and back twisting, she was unloading them from the back of her SUV.

"They deliver this stuff, you know. They even have people who will lay it for you."

"Now you tell me," Lindsay replied curtly over her shoulder.

"Where do you want them?" Moira availed herself, grabbing a few bricks.

Nodding toward the white fir in the middle of the yard, Lindsay directed, "Over there. I'm starting with the big one."

Moira obliged and went back for another load. "You went with Montana flagstone, huh?"

"According to your brother, it's natural, durable and is readily available in my color scheme," Lindsay informed her, setting down her third pile. "Do you want gloves?"

"No, I'm fine."

The two women worked in companionable silence for over an hour, unloading the pavers and stacking them around the trees and flower beds in the front and side yards. Then Lindsay clapped the gray powder off her gloved hands saying, "That's good. I want the border to look random, not manicured."

"Thank God! My back is killing me."

"Consider yourself lucky. My next project is stepping stones down to the water."

"You're on your own there."

They were sitting down in the shade drinking from water bottles when Lindsay noticed the bathing suit ties around Moira's neck. "Oh no! Did we have plans to go to the beach today?"

"No," Moira answered, shaking her head of raven curls. "I just decided to come up. To make sure you were okay."

"I'm fine," Lindsay told her. "Why wouldn't I be?"

"Oh, I don't know. Maybe because you ran into Brian last night. Or because you sounded like you were bouncing off the walls on the phone earlier." She shifted her emerald eyes to the lake, choppy in the late afternoon wind. "Then there was Paul stopping by the office this morning."

"Oh, is he working with you guys again?"

"No. Not yet, anyway," Moira qualified, then shared Lindsay's gaze again. "He's worried about you, about the two of you. He asked me if you really loved him, were marrying him for the right reasons."

Lindsay had to will her voice to sound natural. "And what did you say?"

"I told him to ask you."

Lindsay busied herself with brushing imaginary dust off her jeans as her lifelong friend read her mind.

"Don't worry. He won't."

She returned the presumptive stare. "Why would I worry?"

"Because you're talking yourself into this marriage. I know you and Paul have a history. And that he's madly in love with you, of course. But being in love with someone is different than loving them for a lifetime."

Later it would make sense that guilt registered on Moira's fair face and her eyes grappled with some dilemma, but for now Lindsay's subconscious discounted all of that. "I know. I do love Paul that way."

"If you say so."

Defensive now, Lindsay scooted back a little. "Aren't you the one who told me to stop second-guessing myself and move on?" she contended. "What's done is done and all that."

"I meant about Grace, about coming home to take care of her. That was before Paul proposed. And Brian reappeared."

Lindsay waved the logic away. "It's all the same."

Moira shook her head from side to side. "Your grandmother wasn't the real reason you left San Francisco." She hesitated, then sniffing the air, decided to go on, "And what are the chances of you and Brian being at Hues of Blue at the same time?"

"Coincidence."

"Or fate."

"Fate has not been very kind to me so far. I don't put much stock in it."

"No, I guess you wouldn't," Moira allowed. "Fate can be cruel, has been to you. But like you, it usually has a plan."

Lindsay was utterly confused. "A plan?"

"Whether you knew it or not, you thought Brian would come for you. You thought if you pushed hard enough he'd miss you, give up, give in."

Had she? Lindsay put on her best poker face and refuted briskly, "I didn't have a plan. But either way, he didn't, did he?"

"He didn't ride up on a white horse dressed in shining armor, if that's what you mean." Moira threw a frustrated hand up in the air. "But he did use every portal known to man to try to contact you, including myself. And practically bought out the flower shop in his building."

Lindsay huffed out a dismissive breath as Moira kept going.

"So to justify your behavior, you convinced yourself that he didn't really love you. When you were the one who qualified your feelings, attached the strings, not him."

"We were at a crossroads. I left him a note," Lindsay disputed weakly.

"Yeah, that must have been a great way to top off a long day at the office," Moira fired back. "It was for the best, I suppose. I mean, if you really loved him as much as you'd claimed to, nothing else would have mattered. You wouldn't have felt like you were giving up what you thought your life would be for him."

Lindsay swallowed hard and narrowed her eyes at Moira and her attempt to play the devil's advocate. "And if he really loved me, he would have found me, compromised."

"Compromise is a two-way street. Who's doing the compromising now?" Moira's tone was increasingly cryptic.

Lindsay went with her gut and met it. "Moira, do you have something to say?"

She considered for a moment, then answered quietly, "I love you, Linds. I want you to be happy. But I think you need to ask yourself why you ran away from Brian and why you're marrying Paul. I bet the answer is the same. And it speaks to something greater."

Losing herself in the lake for a few silent beats, Lindsay outwardly ignored the question, but banked it. Instead she informed Moira, "Brian was here this morning. On the beach."

Moira fought a smile, but her dimples betrayed her. "Really?"

Lindsay met her satisfied expression directly. "He didn't come for me. He was here on business."

"Tahoe, yes. The beach, no," she said, closing the small space between them. "No wonder you're stacking stones."

"Yeah," Lindsay told her, lightly tapping Moira's shoulder with hers. "When you didn't pick up I had to do something."

"Sorry. You wanna tell me about it?"

"I'll have to give you the condensed version." Lindsay gauged the sun's position in the sky. "I have to go in and get ready soon. Paul and I have a wedding."

Read on for an excerpt from *Chance Encounter*,
Book Two of the *Chances Trilogy*.

Chance Encounter
The Chances Trilogy Book Two
By Martha O'Sullivan

CHAPTER ONE

It had been ages since Delaney Richards had given a man a second thought, let alone a second look. But the pilot with the hints of gray at the temples of his chestnut-colored hair and smiling eyes had caught her unwitting attention. She watched him greet the oncoming passengers before his gaze found hers and lingered. Then, fever rushing to her cheeks, she pretended to contemplate the baggage handlers loading an adjacent plane. She felt his measured stare for a moment more before he turned away.

"Can I bring you a drink before takeoff?"

Delaney shifted her attention in the direction of the hospitable voice. "Water, please," she told the woman standing over her left shoulder. "Maybe a glass of red wine after takeoff."

The flight attendant shook her head in acknowledgement. "The aisle seat in your row isn't booked. Make yourself comfortable."

Delaney watched her return to the front of the plane and whisper something to the pilot. Nodding in affirmation, he began retreating into the cockpit, but stopped short. His amber eyes met Delaney's and held briefly before he closed the door.

Shaking off the revery, Delaney opened her bag and retrieved her laptop. Being appointed interim vice-president had been a well-deserved yet unexpected promotion. And as luck would have it, she'd been thrown out of the frying pan and into the fire. Rebranding an investment firm with a reputation for tolerating sexual harassment in today's unsparing business climate had been a challenge to say the least. It had consumed her life for the last few months. Her presentation in San Francisco next week could ensure the position became permanent. And she planned to nail it.

She had no sooner brought up the opening slide of her PowerPoint presentation when the flight crew asked for everyone's attention to review the safety procedures. Like most of the passengers, Delaney immediately tuned them out. Until a resounding voice filled the cabin, abruptly pulling her out of work mode.

"Welcome to United Airlines Flight 1126 to San Francisco. This is your captain. We anticipate a smooth four-hour-and-change flight to SFO this evening. I'll update you along the way about our progress as well as point out any landmarks of note below. Thanks for flying with us. Enjoy the flight. We've got the best crew in the business with us tonight."

The next thing she knew, the flight attendant was back at her elbow again. "Not only do you have your row to yourself, but we've got the good California wine tonight." She handed Delaney a glass and a cocktail napkin. "This must be your lucky day."

Delaney returned the smile as the other woman took her leave. Maybe it was. Maybe her luck was finally starting to change.

*****

Even after twenty-plus years behind the stick Captain Mike Savoy never took a smooth landing for granted. Technical check behind him, he exchanged pleasantries with the flight crew before going out into the cabin to thank the passengers for their business.

But tonight his motivation was admittedly twofold. He wanted to see the woman in first-class again. She'd been asleep when he'd left the cockpit mid-flight, and he'd surprised himself by pausing to study her. He hadn't seen her on the countless Chicago to San Francisco flights he'd commanded in the last few years.

"Joining us for dinner, Mike?"

He reluctantly shifted his gaze from the brunette to the blonde staring at him hopefully. Shaking his head, he gave her a closemouthed smile. "Not tonight. I've got some paperwork to catch-up on before I'm out of here."

"I'll wait for you, have a drink until you're done."

Mike sensed the innuendo in the voice of the woman almost young enough to be his daughter. He had a strict no mixing business with pleasure policy. And Caitlin would definitely be pleasure. "You guys go on," he told her. "Maybe next time."

"All right." He felt Caitlin's eyes trail his to the only remaining passenger in the first-class cabin. "You have my cell in case you change your mind." She stepped aside, allowing the cleaning crew to enter before lifting the handle of her wheeled bag. "Good night."

"Good night," Mike threw over his shoulder. The woman had flawless olive skin and her lips shimmered with the same shade of pink gloss that glazed her fingernails. Holding the phone in the crook of her shoulder, she was writing furiously on an envelope. He looked on as she disconnected, then slipped the phone into her enormous purse and stood. Mike nearly tripped over his feet trying to reach her before she slid her carry-on out of the overhead compartment.

"Let me get that." Reaching over her head, he grabbed the bag. It was heavier than he expected. "Long trip?"

"Just a week or so," she answered with a bright smile. "I've been through the lost luggage nightmare twice. I've learned to carry all the essentials with me."

She was so naturally, effortlessly beautiful, Mike couldn't imagine she needed much. "I hope our airline didn't lose your luggage," he remarked.

"No." Her silky hair rested just below her shoulders and her eyes paralleled its dark hue. "Neither time," she hastened to inform him.

"Good to hear."

Their gaze held for a moment more. Then she broke it by saying, "Thank you." She started to reach for the bag.

"This is awfully heavy. I'll carry it out for you."

"That's not necessary. I can get it."

"I insist." Mike extended his arm, gesturing for her to walk ahead of him.

She obliged, walking toward the exit on excruciatingly long legs. She stopped at the breezeway and started to say something, but the roar of the vacuums foiled it. She followed his silent direction and when they reached the gate said, "Thanks."

"My pleasure." Mike found himself oddly compelled to make conversation. "Is San Francisco your final destination?" He was torn between not wanting to let her go and not wanting her to miss a connection.

"Yes, I'm in town for a wedding. I also have some business meetings planned for next week. I don't get out to the West Coast very often anymore."

"Anymore?"

"I went to school out here." She sent an expectant glance down to the bag Mike was still holding. "Thank you again, Captain."

He wanted to ask her where, but her tone had become businesslike and he sensed she was ready to be on her way. "Of course. And it's Mike. Mike Savoy." He set the bag at her feet. She smelled as good as she looked.

"Delaney Richards." She extended her hand. "It's nice to meet you, Mike."

"Likewise." Her hand felt as silky smooth as her hair looked. He found himself wanting run his hands through it just to make sure. "Where are you staying?"

The random question seemed to surprise her as much as it had him. "The Fairmont," she informed him.

"Along with being beautiful, you have excellent taste. You can't go wrong there."

"So I've heard." She blushed a little. "Well, I should get to baggage claim before my suitcase goes to lost and found."

Mike laughed without opening his mouth. "You are a seasoned traveler, Ms. Richards."

"Delaney. And yes, I am. The East Coast and Europe for the most part."

"I've traveled the world myself. But there's no place quite like San Francisco." He handed her the bag. "Enjoy your stay."

"I will."

He watched her disappear into the sea of people. He'd never taken such interest in a passenger before. Not that she seemed to mind. She was traveling alone and not wearing an engagement or wedding ring. Maybe he would see her again on her outbound flight. Or better yet in the city. After all, the Fairmont was only a few blocks from his apartment on Nob Hill.

*****

It was after midnight Chicago time when Delaney arrived in her room. But thanks to her cross-country nap, she wouldn't be going to sleep anytime soon. Gazing at the lights meandering up and down Telegraph Hill, she was reminded of how much she loved San Francisco. The clanking of cable cars and bellowing of foghorns brought her back to the days before impossible deadlines, endless meetings and most of all, a broken heart. Of all the things she'd imagined going wrong on her wedding day, finding herself alone at the altar hadn't made the list.

And she hadn't been anywhere near a wedding since.

There'd been plenty of invitations in the last two years, of course. All of which she'd found a convenient reason to decline. But this one was different. This was Lindsay.

They'd gone from randomly assigned roommates to fast friends in college. Lindsay and Delaney instantly bonded over a myriad of commonalities. Most notably not having a father in their lives, albeit for completely different reasons. Lindsay had lost her parents as a child; Delaney had never known her father. Which made it all the more peculiar that he'd been coming to mind so much lately. She was pushing down the past again when Lindsay's ringtone interrupted her thoughts.

"Welcome back to California." The joy in her friend's voice was palpable.

"Thanks. It's good to be back. How's the bride?

"Better now that the winds have calmed. The smoke from the brush fires in the foothills made its way up here. Keep your fingers crossed that Saturday will be clear."

"Either way everything will be beautiful," Delaney reassured her.

There was dead air for a long moment, then Lindsay said, "It means so much to me that you came, Laney."

Delaney felt her eyes well with tears. But at least her stomach didn't clench anymore. Or threaten to empty. "I wouldn't miss it for the world," she told her and meant it.

"Can you drive up first thing? That way we can catch-up before everything gets crazy tomorrow night."

"Sure." Delaney assessed her reflection in the full-length mirror with a self-deprecating grimace. "I could use a little Tahoe sun."

"That can be arranged. I was afraid you'd be delayed. Fog shut down SFO for a few hours. You were lucky to have gotten in on time."

She felt a a smile sneak in and reverse the crescent moon-like frown on her mouth. "Yeah, today must be my lucky day."

CHAPTER TWO

The morning sunlight streaming through Mike's bedroom window woke him despite the pillow covering his head. He'd been in the air more than not these last few weeks and had been looking forward to some sleep. So much for that. He grabbed a sweatshirt and went to the kitchen to make coffee. While it brewed, he leafed through a week's worth of mail, assessing what needed to be addressed before the weekend with a operose sigh. This last rotation had been a decidedly long haul. Steaming mug in hand, he scooped up the pertinent mail and went outside. Both sets of French doors opened onto a small deck and today Mike chose the one facing east. He sank into the deck chair as the caws of seagulls and the hum of traffic filled the air. Resting his gaze on the Fairmont, he wondered what Delaney Richards was doing this fine morning.

She'd mentioned being in town for a wedding, presumably this weekend, but didn't say how long into next week she'd be staying. Or whom she'd be staying with, he reminded himself with a grunt. Surely such a beautiful woman wouldn't be at loose ends at a wedding. He was still mulling that over when Bruce Springsteen's gravelly voice filled the air.

"Mr. Savoy?"

"Speaking."

"This is the Hyatt Hotel and Casino Lake Tahoe, calling to confirm your Presidential Suite reservation for tonight."

"That's right." Mike consulted his watch. "I should be there around five o'clock. You have my credit card number for the deposit."

"Yes, that's all been taken care of. I understand this is a bachelor party. There is nothing to indicate that refreshments," the caller cleared his throat as if speaking in code, "or anything else is scheduled to be delivered to the room. Are you planning to enjoy the gaming and restaurants on the property? Or can we bring everything to you, perhaps?"

Chuckling, Mike put the man out of his misery. "That won't be necessary." He was long over that kind of bachelor party as was the groom. "There will only be a few of us. The rehearsal dinner is being held on the property as well, at Hues of Blue. We'll be doing some gambling afterwards. There's no live entertainment, per se."

There was a relieved sigh on the other end of the line. "Very good then. We'll look forward to seeing you this afternoon and accommodating you for the next few days."

Mike responded in kind, then reverted his eyes to the Fairmont. He would probably be too busy over the weekend to give Delaney Richards a second thought. But just in case, he'd better decide where to ask her to dinner when he got back.

*****

Watson Brewer had done his due diligence, but a picture was worth a thousand words. And he didn't want to head up to Folsom until he had something concrete. His plan had been to hop on a plane to Chicago, kill two birds with one stone. But the old lady alone wasn't worth the trek. It was the girl. For a guy who hadn't seen his kid in two decades, Colton Richards sure yapped about her a lot, he snickered to himself. He nodded to the man in the red suit trimmed in gold and opted for the revolving door. The lobby lived up to its reputation, but didn't compare to the Bellagio or the Venetian by a long shot.

"Welcome to the Fairmont. Checking in, sir?"

Watson flashed his best smile. "Just visiting a guest. Delaney Richards. I've forgotten the room number."

"It's against hotel policy to give out room numbers, but I can confirm if the guest is registered. You can use the house phone to contact her." The woman half his age punched at the keyboard on the opposite side of the massive oak desk. Then her smile gave way to a frown. "I'm sorry. Ms. Richards checked out this morning."

Watson swore under his breath, but kept his calculated smile bright. "I'm sure she said she'd be in town through the weekend."

"Perhaps she had a last minute change of plans."

Not according to his source at the airline. He ground his teeth, but didn't let the frustration color his voice. "How odd that she wouldn't have mentioned it. Could there be another reservation?"

The clerk narrowed her eyes in suspicion. "That information is confidential. But if you leave your card, I can pass it along should Ms. Richards return."

"That won't be necessary. I'll find another way to contact her," he replied smoothly. "Thanks for checking." He turned on his heel and retraced his steps, feeling her skeptical stare on his back. Stepping out into the midmorning sunshine, he reached into his jacket pocket and pulled out the photograph. She sure was pretty. Pretty enough to be noticed. He shifted his gaze to the doorman, helping an elderly woman out of a taxi. He'd hoped to fly in a little lower on the radar than that. Questions raise more questions, he reminded himself. And he wanted to be the only one asking them.

*****

Lake Tahoe sparkled like diamonds under the boundless blue sky as Delaney entered Incline Village. The estate-like homes shrouded by towering pine trees were as large as the apartment building she'd grown up in, she reminded herself in awe. Reaching her destination, she threw the rental SUV into park and took a couple of deep breaths. She was giving herself props for making it this far when a tap on the window startled her. The eyes looking back at her were as cobalt a blue as the lake itself and the grin as wide as its breadth. Delaney felt the butterflies in her stomach start to settle as she opened the door and stood. Lindsay took her into a warm embrace and hugged her so tight that the two women rocked in place.

"Let me look at you," Lindsay said by way of greeting, giving Delaney a thorough once-over. "Gorgeous as ever, but a little too thin."

"You sound like my mother. I do eat."

With a skeptical squint, she dropped an arm around Delaney's shoulders and led her up the flagstone paved path. "We'll have to work on that this weekend. I can't wait to catch-up. We'll get your bag later."

They reached the two-tiered deck lined with red and white impatiens. "The blue will have to be sky," Lindsay said, reading Delaney's mind. "Note to self, it's impossible to find blue annuals."

"You did all of this yourself?" She took in the perfectly manicured yard, bursting with plants and flowers of all sizes and colors. "When you said you were gardening, I figured you meant a few pots."

"I had to channel my nervous energy somehow. It became a labor of love." Lindsay gestured to one of the chairs circling a slate top table. "Sit. I'll get us something to drink."

"I've been sitting for four hours," Delaney countered, walking to the edge of the deck and imbibing the fresh mountain air. "I'll be right here."

"Suit yourself," Lindsay tossed over her shoulder, blonde ponytail swinging like a pendulum on the back of her head.

Feeling more relaxed than she had in recent memory, Delaney contemplated the water lapping the fawn-colored shore. Her gaze was shifting upward, where rows of pines and aspens dotted the Sierras like soldiers standing at attention when Lindsay returned.

"Amazing how it looks the same, isn't?" Standing next to her, Lindsay handed Delaney a glass of iced tea. "No matter how long you've been away."

"It's magnificent." Delaney took a sip. "A sight for sore eyes from high-rises and strip malls."

"You have a lake in Chicago too, if I remember correctly," Lindsay pointed out with humor shining in her eyes.

"Not like this. I feel like I'm in another world. The air is so crisp, so clean."

"Speaking of clean." Shooting Delaney an pointed stare over the rim of her glass, Lindsay said, "Time for you to."

Delaney played dumb. "Time for me to what?"

"To come clean. You're still not yourself. I could hear it in your voice every time we spoke. What's going on?"

"Nothing's going on," Delaney shot back inadequately.

"Maybe that's the problem. Have you had a night out lately?"

"I'm going to have one tonight, aren't I? And tomorrow night as well."

"I mean a night out with a man." Delaney opened her mouth to speak, but Lindsay barreled over her. "Not business-related. How long has it been?"

"I don't know." Delaney's glance momentarily escaped to the sanctity of the rustic, craftsman-style house. "Is Brian around? I'm dying to meet him."

"He's in Reno picking up his daughter at the airport. Stop trying to change the subject." Lindsay's eyes softened as she went on. "It hurts me to see you like this, letting your life go by. If Ryan walked in here right now, would you forgive him and take him back?"

"No, of course not," Delaney said and meant it.

"Then what are you waiting for? How many dates have you turned down?"

Delaney took a tasteless sip of tea. "None."

"None?" Lindsay amazed. "Are all the men in Chicago blind? Or married?"

"Hardly," Delaney began with a grunt. "I don't really have the time or desire to date. Didn't you feel that way too?"

Lindsay looked away as if mentally rewinding time, then replied heedfully, "Yes, Brian and I both felt that way. That's the difference. Ryan has gone on with his life. You need to do the same." She hesitated, then placing both glasses on the top of the deck railing, took Delaney's hands in hers. "He's not coming back for you, Laney."

"I know." Delaney fixed her eyes on the brown ski runs breaking up the verdant hills. "I realized that even before he eloped." She heaved a sigh. "I don't want him to. I guess somewhere along the way I gave up on true love."

"I did too. So much so that I almost married Paul." She turned Delaney by the shoulders to face her and looked her square in the eye. "I understand what it feels like to love someone that much and lose them. But what you had with Ryan wasn't true love. So your true love is out there somewhere, waiting for you."

*****

Mike pushed the elevator call button repeatedly, frustrated with himself for getting a late start. Lindsay would be frantic by the time he got to the restaurant. Normally he would revel in getting under her skin, but this was different. As was going to a wedding without a date. Even if he and Jessica hadn't called it quits, he wouldn't have asked her to fly in. There were several women he might have asked if the wedding had been in San Francisco.

But this was a weekend, not an evening. Too complicated.

Being in Tahoe again, however, was not complicated. Much of his childhood had been spent here, swimming in the lake in the summer and skiing through forests of frost-painted trees in the winter. He'd been thinking about diversifying his investments and buying a place up here would definitely complement his portfolio.

He walked briskly through the lobby, making mental notes of the casino's layout for later. The last fringes of daylight were sliding behind the milky-white peaks of the Sierra Nevadas as he made his way through the lakeside restaurant. He put on an apologetic frown and clasped Brian's shoulders from behind. "Sorry I'm late."

Brian rose and took Mike into a brotherly hug. "No problem. We're just getting started."

"Hi, Uncle Mike," came a soft voice from the table.

Mike bent down and kissed Brian's daughter on the cheek. "Hi, yourself. How's the most beautiful sophomore at USC?"

"I don't know. I'm a technically a junior after the summer session."

"That's impossible. Just last week you were playing Barbies in my living room," he teased. Secretly, that gave Mike pause.Kelsey had grown into a beautiful girl, the splitting image of her mother, with sable hair to Brian's blonde and hazel eyes to his blue.

Brian shifted his proud gaze to the rest of the table. "Mike, you remember Moira Brody."

"Of course." Mike extended his hand to the fair-faced woman with a headful of black ringlet curls. "Nice to see you again."

Instead of shaking it, she jumped up and embraced Mike from across the table. "You too," she replied, emerald eyes sparkling.

The man beside her stood and offered his hand. "Paul Webster. Nice to meet you."

Mike responded in kind and a silent message passed between them. Then his eyes swept the table draped in white linen and glistening china. "Where's Lindsay?"

"Ladies room. She was getting a little restless waiting for the best man," Brian told him with a chuckle in his eyes. "If you don't want wine, go order a beer. My tab is open."

Nodding in affirmation, Mike headed over to the mahogany bar. Brian had the best table in the house tonight, directly in front of the ceiling-to-floor window wall. When Mike looked beyond it, he saw a fire pit surrounded by Adirondack chairs and wooden benches. He was debating how far the deck extended onto the beach when he heard a familiar voice call his name.But when Mike turned around, he found the last person he could have expected. He felt his jaw drop, then blinked hard a few times, assuming she would disappear or morph into someone else.

But she didn't.

Then he realized Lindsay was hugging him. "You made it," she said. "I was getting a little nervous." She broke away and gestured to the woman at her side. "Mike, this is—"

"Delaney Richards," he managed to finish for her.

Lindsay's gaze sliced between them in awe. "You two know each other?"

"I brought her plane in last night."

"And carried my bag out to the gate for me," Delaney added.

"This is the wedding you flew in for?"

A warm smile replaced the astonishment in her eyes. "Lindsay was my roommate in college."

"Brian is my next door neighbor."

"You're the best man?"

Mike could do nothing but nod.

They were still beholding each other when Lindsay cleared her throat and interjected, "Well, I'd better get back to the table." She directed her parting words at Delaney. "I'll meet you there. Take your time."

Delaney's lips parted slightly and she watched Lindsay walk away, as if unsure whether to follow. Not wanting her to, Mike instantly stepped forward. "Can I get you a drink?" She smelled intoxicating; spicy and sexy, akin to the strapless dress she wore.

"No thanks," she declined, meeting his gaze again. "I have a glass of wine at the table."

Mike simply could not take his eyes off of her. After a long moment, Delaney suggested, "We should probably get back there too."

Mike grabbed his beer from the bar and extended his arm. "After you."

She complied, seemingly unaware of the male heads turning to undress her with their eyes as she walked toward the table. Of which Mike was one.

She turned, as if sensing he wasn't behind her, and cocked her head to the side with a puzzled expression. "Mike? Are you coming?"

Mike shook off the stupor and made quick work of the space between them. Then, placing his hand at the small of her back without touching her, he guided her across the room.

There were still three vacant chairs at the table, one with a bird's-eye view of the water and the mountains and two on the opposite side, facing the restaurant. Delaney stopped in front of one of the latter and addressed Kelsey, "Am I losing it, or did you move?"

Before Kelsey could respond, Lindsay piped up. "I asked her to scoot over so we could chat. You don't mind, do you?"

"Of course not." Delaney replied, starting to pull out one of the chairs.

Mike beat her to it. "Here," he offered hurriedly as their arms brushed. He wondered if she'd also felt the dizzying twinge.

"Thanks." She tossed him a look from under her lashes and sat down. And without a second's debate Mike took the chair next to her, opting for the better view.